What Poets Need

What Poets Need

Finuala Dowling

PENGUIN BOOKS

PENGUIN BOOKS

Published by the Penguin Group
80 Strand, London WC2R 0RL, England
Penguin Putnam Inc, 375 Hudson Street, New York, New York 10014, USA
Penguin Books Australia Ltd, 250 Camberwell Road, Camberwell,
Victoria 3124, Australia
Penguin Books Canada Ltd, 10 Alcorn Avenue, Toronto, Ontario,
Canada M4V 3B2
Penguin Books (NZ) Ltd, Cnr Rosedale and Airborne Roads, Albany,
Auckland, New Zealand
Penguin Books India (P) Ltd, 11 Community Centre, Panchsheel Park,
New Delhi – 110 017, India
Penguin Books (South Africa) (Pty) Ltd, 24 Sturdee Avenue, Rosebank,
Johannesburg 2196, South Africa

Penguin Books (South Africa) (Pty) Ltd, Registered Offices:
24 Sturdee Avenue, Rosebank, Johannesburg 2196, South Africa

First published by Penguin Books (South Africa) (Pty) Ltd 2005

'Spam' © Finuala Dowling first appeared in Off-The-Wall Poetry, 2003
'Why my life is like Retreat Station' © Finuala Dowling first appeared in
Carapace 46
'Cecil Beaton is not dead enough' © Finuala Dowling first appeared in
scrutiny2, vol 2, no 1, 2003

ISBN 0 143 02468 X

Typeset by DW Design in 11/13 pt Bodoni
Printed and bound by Interpak Books, Pietermaritzburg
Cover design: Flame Design, Cape Town

For the women in my life
– Beaty, Ma, Biddy, Tessa and Cara –
who gave me the time

I know how poems are made.

There is a place the loss must go.
There is a place the gain must go.
The leftover love.

from Alice Walker
How Poems Are Made/A Discredited View

When you are not there, I don't know who I am. The happiness of each day is poised around the arrival of your letter.

It usually comes at four in the afternoon. At 3.45 I start to make a tray of tea. This is a hungry time of day for me, and I used to make toast, too (a raisin bun, squashed flat and blackened in the toaster, fatly layered with butter), but Steve my computer guy pointed out the disgusting amount of debris wedged into my keyboard, so now I eat something in the kitchen and bring just the tea here. Though even that I spill.

The anticipation is partly the simple pleasure of the company of your words. To walk with you and your dogs in the shady wind-breaks of the farm, listening to their eerie whispering hum. To swim with you in the clay-bottomed dam among frogs. To feel the warmth of the enclosed space and smell the young buds as you walk into the tunnel every morning. To drink austere black tea with you. To listen to you saying wise, soothing things to Jackie or Liza when they phone about their latest man crisis. To sit with you on your stoep in the evening, thinking your thoughts with you.

Those thoughts are always plans of goodness. The truth is that ever since you got the prize for *esprit de corps* at Queenstown Girls' High School in 1974, you have felt the mantle of perpetual devotion. Perhaps some wild child, son of friends of yours, needs expensive drug rehabilitation and you agonise over how to give them a big loan that they won't feel pressed to repay. Or perhaps one of your rose-pickers is being abused by

1

her husband: it falls to you to get her a new life. And then the perennial Frikkie, whom you first encountered being perambulated in a shopping trolley, has some fresh request. You're always bailing out the needy, setting off their losses against your gains. Though sometimes I fear the purity of your thoughts, still I look forward to them. Saint Theresa.

But another part of me anticipates something else. Perhaps today she'll write that she's leaving Theo at last. That she's asked for a divorce. That she's coming to me. That he's dead.

We no longer lie to each other. I don't think we ever did. But there was a time when I didn't say all the brutal things I thought. As I've just done. We used to leave things out.

I try to wait till 4.05 to log on. I want your mail to be there already. If Outlook Express says, Receiving message 1 of 12, then I think, Good, there are at least eleven chances that Theresa's is one of these. When I see your name, the universe is benign. I quickly delete the spam so that you are not defiled by proximity to the rapacious beasts. I sink into your words. I'm bowled over by you afresh. I don't even mind that Theo is not dead.

Theo says that the Isuzu's engine is completely wrecked, pistons cracked, crankshaft driven backwards through some vital aspect, you write, and he has gone to Caledon to see if Dieselman Henry has a solution. Then I love you for being alone on the farm, for moving about in a world of pistons and crankshafts, for the phrase 'vital aspect', and for knowing or naming 'Dieselman Henry'.

When it is not there (though it almost always turns out you've faithfully sent it, it has just got trapped in a cyber backlog) I am mean, I am vindictive. I take each one of the eleven spams inviting me to enlarge my penis,

2

get cheap drugs, get rich quick and lose weight, and I click Properties, Message Source, highlight and copy and paste them into a mail which I send off to my service provider under the header Abuse. I used to imagine that this resulted in punitive action, spammers in Wyoming opening their front doors to a posse of cleansing police, who would confiscate their hard drives and wash out their mouths with soap. But Steve says I must be nuts; probably my service provider just deletes my whinges. He says Wyoming is a very beautiful state.

Today there will be no letter, I know, just spam. And the twelfth letter, which is always Ryno's. I can rest assured that even if your mail is held back, Ryno's will come powering through, like Ryno himself, hacking through some Malayan jungle or trudging in crampons through Himalayan snow, Ryno reporting to me in terse one-line emails from the land of real men. My friend has another side to him, of course; everyone does. But hacking and trudging are on the dust jacket.

Every year, as August approaches, I know that it will happen. You don't mention it beforehand, don't build up a picture of the preparations, the booking, or the packing, but I know that soon I'll receive the one that begins: 'This will be my last mail until September. Theo and I drive to Johannesburg tomorrow and stay the night with Jackie. Then our usual holiday in the Kruger National Park. I'll miss you.'

I can't bear it that you are going on holiday with your husband. Why do you have to go on holiday to the same place you honeymooned? Why this sentimental pilgrimage? I hate the way you are both interested in baobab trees. I wish that one of you were restless for a casino, or even an acacia. I hate the thought of your happy family reunions with your daughters. I hate your campfires. I am shut out, my nose pressed to the pane, dribbling with envy. I don't even belong in the same room as a happily married couple.

Are you happily married?

Ways of Keeping
I have kept my love for you
like an unloved dog,
chained up in the yard.

You have kept your love for me
pressed between
pages of a well-loved book.

With a diamond you have secretly
etched your love for me into a glass pane,
showing me its hiding place
with a cupped hand.

One night, unable to sleep for thoughts of you, I got up and scribbled this down with a pale pencil crayon on a scrap of paper. I've just broken it into lines, choosing to put 'pages' on a new line and omitting the definite article. I do take line breaks seriously, don't adhere to the carriage-return theory of poetry.

There is definitely something still wrong in the last stanza. It still has the heavy sign-pointing of prose. You can even see that the second line is too long. Rather: 'You have etched/ your love for me into glass', but that would take away the faint echo of 'pain' in 'pane'. 'You have secreted your love for me/ etched it in a pane'? But 'diamond' is good. Leave it, they say, put it in a drawer

4

and come back to it.

No, I know:

> With a diamond you have secretly
> etched ~~your love for~~ me into a glass pane,
> showing me ~~its~~ ^{my} hiding place
> with a cupped hand.

And maybe also make the tense less perfect:

> With a diamond you ~~have~~ secretly?

You have gone away, and when you come back, you won't tell me about your holiday. You told me once, just a little, about the game park trip. But I behaved badly. I raged about the campfires and the stars. I imagined Theo whispering to you to see the lioness and her cubs or some other rustling intimacy of the savannah. So now you spare me, and even the sparing is painful.

Today I walked a very long way, across the saddle of Kalk Bay mountain by way of Echo Valley, down past the old silver mine itself, up onto Ou Kaapse Weg, past the woodcutters with their bundles of rooikrans, all the way to a mechanic's workshop behind the old Sun Valley shopping mall. My car has been in for repairs – it's been overheating, has had its pressure checked and its system flushed but still the gauge swung up and the rusty looking water boiled. At last a cracked cylinder gasket has been diagnosed and has been sealed with metal stitching.
    Beth would have given me a lift, or I could have caught the train and a taxi, or walked along the main road and across the avenues, but I chose this three-hour route.

The weather was crisp, one of those brilliant, blue-skied late winter days when the peninsula seems to apologise for unremitting rain.

As I hiked, focused on my destination but alive to the fynbos and sugarbirds around me, I thought of a friend who once outlined the plot of a novel he planned to write about Cape Town. Various disasters would befall the city, resulting in a massive drop in population and necessitating a gradual return to nineteenth and even eighteenth century forms of transport: steam train, horse-drawn carriage, sailing boat. One of the last big tankers would dock at Simon's Town and load derelict, obsolete motor vehicles for shipment to the Far East. Pristine nature would return. Dull parking areas in Fish Hoek would be reclaimed by the dune system, tarred roads would decay and eventually be wrenched up, leaving the sandy track of history. The bend between Kalk Bay and Clovelly would revert to a perilously rocky set of steps requiring assistance in descent, and consequently the re-establishment of the old corner toll.

Once I had listened to this detailed outline – not really a plot, but a beautifully imagined setting – I knew that my friend would never write the book. Because if a writer starts letting out his ideas before he puts pen to paper, they escape, taking their energy with them. This is particularly true if the plot outline or germinal idea is met with rapturous interest. On the other hand, I have noticed on two occasions when I outlined ideas for poems and was met by blank stares, I went back and wrote them with uncanny force, as if to say, See, fool, this is what I meant! Perhaps these observations of mine are true not just of artistic plans.

I never know if what I say to you is obvious, something you and everybody else have always known, and I only just lighted upon.

It's interesting to me that I walked that distance today with ease. I have developed a taste for exercise relatively late in my life. My infantile aversion to physical recreation I put down to the fact that duffers, weaklings, boys without Springbok colours potential, were actively discouraged from partaking in games in my youth.

In my youth.

It was all about winning. If one wasn't good at them, one had no place in games. Then in the army, exercise was only ever a form of punishment, an excellent way to break you down so that you could be re-created in the image of the SADF.

After I *klaared* out, I got into the habit of not taking exercise. In my late twenties I would have been puffed by the first leg of today's hike and prayed for mountain rescue. Now, at thirty-seven, having happily discovered the truth that moving one's limbs in a coordinated yet non-competitive manner is a simple human pleasure, the hike was exhilarating. I note without comment that the boys who were first-team rugby, cricket etc, even *victor ludorum* Ryno himself, are nursing ominous knee and shoulder injuries these days.

I took water with me on my excursion, and cheese and tomato sandwiches. I'd have liked to carry nothing but a biscuit in my pocket, as Mr Ramsay claims to have done in his youth, but I'm made of more mortal stuff. Or maybe the 'biscuit' Mr Ramsay refers to was pemmican.

When I got back, the sun was starting its early afternoon descent behind the mountain. It's more of a sudden drop than a descent. Unlike the Atlantic seaboard, we do not enjoy lingering sunsets. But I could see the Brass Bell still basking in a sunny patch so I went down with a newspaper and had two beers on the wooden decks, catching the occasional spray of the rising tide. You can see our house from down there: from a distance it has a certain Edwardian, bow-fronted, St-Ives-ish charm.

A word came to me to describe myself: insouciant. I know it's come to be associated more and more often with its pejorative meaning, 'unconcerned' (see INDIFFERENCE, says my dictionary), but I prefer 'carefree'. I am carefree because I have a half-share in a valuable seaside property; the Feinstein Trust has sent me my contract; I live my life at my own pace. Though I miss you, and long for you, it is also true that without this mood of yearning, I would not be able to write any poetry.

I read somewhere that the British poet laureate Andrew Motion once took or sometimes takes cough mixture in order to simulate the slightly sorry-for-yourself head cold feeling so conducive to verse.

I'm feeling drowsy after those beers.

Please don't think that I am comparing you to cough syrup.

Sunday 11th August
7.15 pm

This morning I bit into an apple and was filled with disappointment and something else, like hankering. The apple was small with a dull, soapy taste that spoke of cold storage. It called itself Golden Delicious when it was neither. What could I expect from a Value Pack?

I remembered the day we walked through the orchards

till we reached the older, more venerable trees. You picked a big, shiny red, polished it on your jeans and said, 'Taste this. South Africans don't usually get this quality – they're all exported.' The apple was crunchy and intensely sweet; juice dribbled down my chin at the first bite. I was telling you how delicious the taste was – always difficult to find the right words when one's mouth is full – when it occurred to me that you had intended this moment. You knew when we set out for this apparently casual stroll – 'Come, I'll show you the farm's boundaries' – that you would stop at a tree familiar to you and get me to taste a real apple. We were not lovers, not yet, but we were doing what lovers do, that shy sharing of favourite things. I looked into your eyes until you looked away and summoned the dogs to heel. I was sure you were thinking about me, and this pleased me immensely. But it turned out that, as always, you had been struck by some thought about the needy.

'I want Theo to give this orchard to the workers, for them to harvest and develop on their own.'

I am so wrapped up in myself: you are almost completely unravelled in the service of others. You were, I think, denied self-pity from the very start, when you stood stoically, five years old, on Cathcart station waiting for the train to Queenstown where you were to be a termly boarder. Your three older sisters knew how everything worked: the timetable, the coaches, the seats, the new term. They hailed old friends and messed about with hockey sticks. Your dashing father and willowy mother stood arm-in-arm, still terribly in love, perhaps even – heartlessly – looking forward to a childless break. You held your tuck box and were watchful.

It was Sal's first holy communion today, so I made a rare

guest appearance at church. Sal has been looking forward to the white dress and mantilla as much as she has been dreading her first confession. She did the confession last week. God knows what she confessed.

The priest adopted his most ingratiating children's hour tone of voice, speaking of mummies and daddies and how they must give a big hug to kind Mrs O'Leary, their catechism teacher, who had brought them to God's great red checked tablecloth. I'm so tired of these worldly priests. Here is my message to all novitiates: I don't want to hear your petty prejudices. I don't want to know about the cake sale or whether Team A or Team B is cleaning the windows this week. I want you to stand there and let God course through you to me. Go get me God. Otherwise, become a floor manager at the hypermarket, or find yourself a car park to guard.

I leafed through the missal, thinking how all my childhood I heard these beautiful words spoken; their cadences and images – of that which is bound and that which is loosed, of those who look without seeing, of captors who ask for songs, of the vine and its branches, of the last become first, of He who will come after me and baptise with the holy spirit and with fire. *And with fire.* How my namesake must have relished the power in that. Surely these phrases entered me and stayed, like a template?

I don't know why Beth is bringing Sal up as a Catholic when she was so vociferously against the Church as a teenager. Is it true that we all eventually revert to form? I don't think so. Beth sent Sal to Holy Cross because it is close by, and because it is still small and run on principles of kindness, as it was in Beth's day. Then I suppose it was simply a natural development that Sal, watching the teachers crossing their breasts with holy water, would ask to be part of that secret society of ritual and beauty, the cabbala that had already taught her to recite those deeply patterned prayers that never go away, even if one majors in sociology: Our Father; Hail Mary; The angel of the Lord declared; Hail Holy Queen; I confess to Almighty God; Holy, holy, holy; Through Him, with Him, in Him; Peace be with you; Go in peace.

Beth is not quite right these days. She's always been excessively active and efficient (she wears dungarees a lot), but lately there's been something manic about her domestic and professional preoccupations. I'll catch her coming upstairs with a pile of laundry, at the same time talking on her cellphone to a client, while nodding or shaking her head at Sal's questions about whether cows are born with teeth and has she ever seen a ghost. Beth stands in front of the linen cupboard as if she's not sure if she should be putting the sheets or herself inside it.

She's become obsessive about the dilapidation of the house. It's true that some of the front windows, the big ones that look over the bay, we no longer dare to open. Sea salt, constant moisture and years without maintenance have rusted the hinges and rotted the wood so that the slightest tug would leave us toothless, in need of boarding up. And it's not just the windows. 'Stand here, John,' Beth said today. 'Do you feel this floorboard giving in? If only I could get a really big contract, I could get a man in to repair some of these things before we're actually condemned.'

I said I was sorry that poets weren't really tongue-in-groove men, or only metaphorically. She looked at me distractedly and asked how much the Feinstein Trust would be paying me. I said I'd chip in what I could, but who could we get to do it, and at what price? I mean, the damp is actually infiltrating in the first place not just because of the gutters, but because the rain funnels itself right through the brick, in transverse cracks that are quite visible from the outside. Against one particularly bad interior wall we've had to hang a decorative cloth to disguise the impressive crop of fungus we seem to be growing. It's not so much a question of getting a man in as contracting a firm of engineers.

Maybe we could just cover the wonky floor with a layer of chipboard, I said. It's hard for me to face real problems head on. Beth gave me a pained look.

The house depresses Beth, or perhaps adds to an existing depression. I see her getting tearful at the ironing basket, but her tears are not for the floorboards or the window hinges. It isn't her work even, though it may be the pressure of being a single parent on top of running a drafting and design business. Beth complains that her life is just drudgery, all work and motherhood. I said she really should take more evenings off; I'm here, I can take care of Sal. Beth said who would she go out with? Hadn't I heard there were no single straight men in Cape Town? As she's my sister, I didn't take offence. Then she felt bad about her sarcasm and thanked me, saying she was so tired in the evening all she could think about was sleep anyway. I reminded her of her teenage popularity.

'All the boys I kissed in those days,' said Beth, 'all those skateboarders and red-eyed pot smokers, they're all deputy provincial cabinet ministers and pop stars these days.'

I knew which two she meant.

While we were talking about the house falling down and Beth's oscular gift, Sal came in with her language book. Beth said, 'Let your uncle help, he's the linguist.' What she means is that grammar interests me. Sal showed me the lists of collective nouns and stock comparisons she has to learn for a test. A fleet of ships, a litter of puppies, a swarm of bees. As green as grass, sick as a dog, weak as a kitten.

There are two reasons I can't help you with this, I said. One, I refuse to endorse your school's interest in perpetuating clichés. Two, I notice that these pages are all photocopied from textbooks, which is a breach of copyright. Publishing houses go under because of this kind of thing.

Beth grabbed the book away from me. 'Why do you have to be so damn clever all the time? Why can't you do a simple thing and just help her with her homework? All you do is write poetry or think about writing poetry and look after number one!' She swept Sal away from me.

I felt bad. We've never been a fighting family. After twenty minutes I went into Beth's bedroom where the two of them were revising flocks of geese but probably not coveys of grouse, exultations of larks or watches of nightingales.

I thought I'd bake some potatoes in the oven for your supper, I said, and fry some onions before I go out. Is that all right? 'That'll be lovely,' said Beth, 'we'll be down just now to make a salad.' They're down there eating now. I can hear happy mother and daughter laughter.

The thing about Beth is that Ron was such a pointless husband. I think she married him in a gesture of defiance against our upbringing, which was academic bordering on the bohemian. Ron is a tall yet strangely babyish notary and conveyancer who orders lime milkshakes when everyone else is drinking scotch and who thinks the

13

height of wit is to call milk 'cow juice', eggs 'bum nuts' and orange juice 'OJ'. I never saw him when he wasn't claiming to be tired or hungry or both. Ma and I used to joke that we were keeping a bottle of champagne behind sealed glass, with a sign saying 'Break open in case Beth divorces Ron'.

Ron likes to watch. He watches sport and sitcoms and action movies and other people's lifestyles. His big topic of conversation is a friend of his who is very rich and always buying new things. He slurps on his milkshake and his eyes go wide as he describes his friend's flat-screen TV or imported digital camera. Ron would like to be rich and always buying new things, but at the end of the day (as he would say) he prefers to put his feet up on his couch and flick through the channels. He expects to win the lottery; that is another real thing in Ron's life.

When Beth came back here to Quarterdeck Road after three years of marriage, I feared that Ron would pitch up on our doorstep sobbing. But apparently he met her departure with relief. He remarried almost instantly, a very thin woman – Lilian – who always asks me solicitously whether I'm tired, by which I understand that I look hung-over, dishevelled or unshaven and/or that my private love of butter has taken on a public dimension.

Since her divorce, Beth's life has been Sal and her work. Sometimes when we are making supper together, Beth will tell me again that she can't believe her marriage to Ron; is still stunned by it; can't fathom why she did it. Then I say, You got Sal.

14

I am sitting huddled here with a hot water bottle against the icy cold and a great throbbing bandaged thumb: I nearly sliced the tip right off helping Beth make smoked peppered mackerel sandwiches for her guests, who are still here, I think, including the great Johannesburg mogul whose new house plans she has drawn up. It's a huge contract and he's promising her more work, even a retainer, hence the peppered mackerel.

The mogul talks loudly and incessantly, as if his money has bought him more airspace than the rest of us enjoy. He asked me what I did. I said I was a poet. This set him off reciting some lewd limericks. Then he said, 'No, seriously, how do you earn a living?'

I don't normally mind admitting to people that I've only had one permanent job in my life, when I worked for Karoo Books in Jo'burg. There is, after all, an art to being freelance. You have to stay calm in the ninety days it takes for your invoice to be paid. You have to trust that the phone will ring with another editing or proofreading or report writing job before the current one runs out. Since it is likely that two or more contracts will overlap, you have to believe that all deadlines have an afterlife. But I didn't feel that the mogul deserved my insights into the solemn vows of freelancing. So I said, I'm an editor. This didn't ring any bells with him, so he continued to talk about himself.

The problem, I find, with lots of social interaction is the way it wastes precious time that could be spent doing something much more important, like writing a poem, reading a book or catching up on the mundane chores that sometimes inspire poems. You start to wish you had brought a drawer along to tidy up on your lap, as the narrator does in a Dorothy Parker short story we studied at university.

In this spirit, I was more than happy to volunteer to do the sandwiches instead. Beth buys these ultra-sharp Victorinox knives and I was trying to shave the crusts off the sandwiches with one of them when I turned my thumb into sashimi. The blood poured and poured, into the little bowl of ice cubes, all over the basin, into copious paper towels, down my wrist. The pain was intense, ridiculously so. I could feel all the intricate mechanisms – nerves – connecting my finger to my shoulder tingling with outrage. Beth seemed irritated with me, as if I'd done it on purpose. More concerned about the (bloody) sandwiches.

Sal was much more sympathetic. While I staunched, she read to me from our family medical book which says that one can lose up to one fifth of one's blood with no ill effects. The sight of me in extremis raised, for Sal, many questions about God and heaven, some of which she answered herself. For example, Jesus still has brown hair, and while his Father sits on a white throne, Jesus stands less formally at the doors of heaven to welcome newcomers, who arrive all the time, especially children from the Cape Flats and soldiers from the Middle East. She was still wearing her ballet clothes, which added to the surrealism of her theological observations.

What I should be telling you is that today was the first official day of my contract to edit *The Unofficial View*. This morning I sent out an email calling for submissions. I have the private email addresses of about forty South African poets. Then I also despatched notices through the Writer's Network newsletter and Artslink. I felt that I had done something, that I was not dilly-dallying. What else should a new editor do, I thought. I couldn't call a meeting because I have no staff. I tidied my desk in anticipation of the deluge. I tested all my pens and threw out the ones that are drying out or leaking. I wrote a list of all the things I need to do to get the first edition out:

Cover illustration
20-26 poems
List of contributors
Preface/editorial by me
Other illustrations: cartoons/woodcuts?

There didn't seem to be anything else to do, so I went for a walk on Fish Hoek beach, looking across at the sleeping profiles of the Helderberg. Afterwards I drove to Simon's Town where I had coffee and a large toasted egg, bacon and banana sandwich at a little restaurant on Jubilee Square. Most people like weekends, but I like the feeling of an idle Monday, to be at leisure while starched naval officers bustle past about their business. Feeling pleasantly crumpled, I read the paper and a little Japanese novel in translation.

The sandwich made me thirsty so I ordered juice and in this state, full and calm, I thought of you and me. And archy and mehitabel: 'expression is the need of my soul,' wrote archy, hopping from key to key, without capital letters. How I loved that book. My mother said archy and mehitabel were cult figures when she was at university.

I tried to think whereabouts on my shelves I'd find my copy – I haven't looked at it in years. It made me quite agitated. All the way home in the car I tried to picture the cover. It is a later Faber edition, I think, bright yellow with black writing, without a picture. Someone showed me the original 1927 edition once. It has a big cartoon cat against a higgledy-piggledy skyline. How I'd love to own that. At home I went straight to my shelves, but I couldn't find my copy anywhere. I must've lent it to someone who never returned it. Ryno, perhaps, though it's a bit out of date for him. He doesn't really like reading, I suspect, but he likes to be able to refer casually to the title and author of the latest publishing sensation, especially when women are present. I'm never, never, never lending another book out. Except to you. You can take your pick.

I had an afternoon nap because I didn't get my full quota last night. After I'd put the potatoes in for Beth and Sal yesterday evening, and fried the onions, and written to you, I took a quick shower and met Red Moffat and his wife Frances at Cape to Cuba. He'd just heard that he'd won the Roy Campbell prize, and in a celebratory mood we drank too much. Everyone likes Red because he still has this boyish, surfer charm. Lots of surfers are really clever; submitting doctorates on Jung or studying whale skeletons or winning poetry prizes; but the longterm effect of sunburn, of salt water in sinus cavities, anvils and tear ducts, gives them a deceptively glazed look. Red has this look. Anywhere else it might spell derelict or hobo, but in Cape Town (and California, I suspect) it lends grooviness. His face says, 'I'm from here.' The barman at Cape to Cuba knows Red from the reef so he kept sliding us these cocktails called Local Charm in recognition of Red's local hero status.

When we came out of the restaurant, it was late. The streets were wet with rain and deserted. The darkened houses rose above the Victorian shop façades, clinging to the steep hillside, keeping their opinions to themselves.

Then in the midst of the stillness, we saw a group of teenagers running, shrieking in the road. I knew how they felt, it came back to me how it feels to be seventeen. Like this:

Them Only
Past midnight, the street is wide and wet
with night rain. Teenagers come haring,
scaring, down the clean, free, centre lane,
the first and only pioneers to hold and kiss
without permission, to stay up after eleven,
to laugh at nothing, to run five abreast
on the abandoned tar, high on hash or beer
or love, in the streaming mist of witching hour,
when the shops are dark and barred
and all the feds and dads and *laaities*
and school principals and moms in nighties
are fast asleep, having surrendered the world
to them, to youth, to the belly ring girls,
to the cowlick boys with dark-ring eyes,
to them and them only, no one besides.

Beth suspected I might overdo it, so she had left a herbal sachet of something called Sober on my bed. But when I staggered in at 1.30 am, I was so trashed I fell asleep on top of the sachet. All the granules melted together inside the foil from my body heat. As we discovered this morning, when Beth prised the packet apart, looking at me like a matron. I'm all right now, drank lots of juice and told myself I'll never touch a drop again. If there was any alcohol left in my body it poured out of my thumb with the blood just now.

I don't have to go; I'm not dashing off. Too often you end your letters with 'dashing off' or 'must go' or 'left this too late so there's only time for a quick note'. But when I complain, you say that you think of me all the time, that in any case it is I who am the writer, the one who records with ease.

expression is the need of my soul

Of course you're right, what you say is true. I have more time than you do and I live to write. I just want to say that I get jealous that so many people have claims on you and your time, that they all take precedence. If I count Theo and the girls, the dogs, your workers, and your suppliers, I'd be lucky to find that I come twenty-sixth or twenty-seventh in your priorities. The queue is long; I find myself pressing against the others, trying to make it go faster, like the poorer shoppers do at Shoprite Checkers.

Please don't think I'm comparing you to a cashier.

Wednesday 14th August
8.30 am

Let me catch you up on Tuesday's thoughts before Wednesday surges in and blots them out.

A woman approached me on the beach yesterday morning. Actually I saw her on my Monday walk on the rocks at the Clovelly end with her dalmatian, and hoped she wasn't poaching mussels. I never linger down that end because it is so gloomy; almost permanently in the shade from the acclivity above – and because the abandoned railway station, once a fun place to jump on the train without paying, has taken on such an ominous quality. Anyway, just as I was preparing to swing round and face the sunlit Fish Hoek hillside again, this woman came towards me holding out a little wet white feather. Her first words were sucked out with the tide, but her speech ended: '... especially for you, because you are such a lovely man.' I didn't like her, I mean her feyness – the slight tinkle of bells around her ankles – though 'lovely' is better than 'special', and one needs all the affirmation one can get, even from people who burn incense. I told Sal and she said, 'But how did the woman KNOW you were lovely?'

Last week Beth asked if she could leave Sal in my care while she flies to Johannesburg about her big contract, the ersatz mansion for the super-rich businessman, which he now wants her to project-manage. She's not keen but says she'll stay the first ten days or two weeks then maybe fly up from time to time. My job as surrogate mother starts today.

Sal and I will be fine. In pre-school Sal felt a lack of siblings to list to the inquisitive teacher, so she said that in fact, yes, she had a brother, John. She's grown up with me in the house and certainly sees as much of me as she does of Beth, who's always busy, always saying 'Later' to Sal.

It's interesting because I think that's what our mother did to Beth. Beth grew up with this very strong role model. Ma always had a seminar or lecture to prepare, usually on a topic related to the nascent discipline of gender studies. Ma loved Beth's ambition and, in a funny sort of way, my lack of ambition. 'You'll be a writer,' she smiled indulgently, the way I imagine fathers once told their daughters they'd be wives and mothers. I was christened John Stuart Carson after the philosopher who supported women's rights. Beth is really Elizabeth, after any number of eponymous pioneers. It took me a long time to realise why my mother and Beth – both ardent feminists – served my father all his meals on a tray. It was to remind him that he was merely a passenger.

Which reminds me that when Ma died and I inherited her Opel Kadett, I'd still sometimes go out with the keys and absentmindedly get into the passenger seat. I'd sit there for a split second before I remembered that I was the driver. I don't do that any more.

I finished the book *The Key* which was rather weak at the end but otherwise very amusing, though I don't think that was intentional. I bought it because someone in the *Financial Times* weekend supplement mentioned it as their all-time favourite novel. The idea of a demure Japanese wife who can only discover sexual pleasure when she is blind drunk on brandy and practically asleep, with her delighted husband taking Polaroid photographs of her never-before-witnessed naked body and indulging in his foot fetish, really just tweaked my funny bone.

I'm glad I had the book with me yesterday morning in the Olympia café, where I'd stopped for coffee (and scrambled eggs and caramelised tomatoes) on the way back from the beach. There were a couple of guys there whom I vaguely know – I mean, they've grown up around here too, we've rubbed shoulders – and they were talking about their weekend plans. There were lots of women's names being bandied about, some I thought I recognised, attached to pretty faces, and talk of yachts and champagne breakfasts. They were obviously going to have a good time. This strange feeling came over me, of being left out. I don't know why, since they're not my friends, only barest acquaintances; I've certainly never invited them anywhere and I wasn't even sitting at their table. But their talk made me feel both bored and envious, tangled up together. I'd probably hate it on their yacht, and the sea and the champagne would combine to produce nausea. Still, it would be nice to be able to say, And this weekend I've been invited out for a champagne breakfast on a friend's yacht. I could, for instance, say it to you, and you might feel a pang of jealousy, and briefly imagine me suntanned in my shirtsleeves, the wind blowing through my still thick curls while someone urges me to 'Tack!'

Laugh, Theresa. I like it when I make you laugh.

What else to tell you of my Tuesday? Beth and I shared a bottle of Chateau Libertas, which is being sold at a bargain R19.99 at the Lakeside Spar. (I recovered so well from my hangover that I decided to start drinking again.) I made a coriander pesto which we ate with pasta. Tip: use sesame and sunflower seeds instead of macadamia nuts. We read Sal's English composition, about 'The Day I Flew a Hot Air Balloon'. It was a title the whole class had been given. Sal wrote (original spelling): 'I fownd an old hot air balloon in the shed. I was so excited. I lit the fire and it inflated. When I was high up in the sky I looked down and saw Mommy scrubbing the front steps and my uncle John washing his car in the driveway. Then I went over the sea. A bird was flying next to me. It plummetted down to catch a fish.' Beth asked, 'Why didn't you say your mommy was drawing up house plans and your uncle was writing a poem? And where did we get this driveway from?' Sal said she just wanted her life to sound normal.

'Plummeted' is good, I said.

When I went to bed last night I stupidly ignored a

slight itch at the back of my throat. But at night the pollen grains and mould flakes and whatever other allergens there are descend for the kill. After midnight, I found myself desperately sucking on the back of my own throat, trying to use my tongue to scratch this deep itch around my uvula. Eventually I got up, inhaled the nasal spray which I'm supposed to do three times a day but always forget, took two antihistamines and two extra-strength Disprins and fell into a heavy sleep. Today there is a kind of speed bump when I swallow, and I'm constipated.

How close we are.

Wednesday 14th August
11.50 pm

The headless nude is gone, sold, but the ghost of you remains. After dropping Sal at Holy Cross I stopped by the Empire café and remembered the day you met me there. You said, tilting towards the painting above us, 'I wonder why artists sometimes leave the head off? Do they do that with male subjects too?'

I looked at you and said, because the thought struck me then so forcefully, that you are not just pretty. You have the beauty of culmination, that comes from generation upon generation of fine noses marrying limpid eyes, of luminous skin marrying good cheekbones. You laughed and blushed and then you said, 'Other men should come to you for lessons. You could teach other men how to woo.' Then you reached across and grasped my wrist, a rare public moment in an otherwise profoundly secret and often shamefully furtive archive.

Now I have it! 'Ways of Keeping' must have an ending that comes back to its beginning. Thus:

Ways of Keeping
I have kept my love for you
like an unloved dog,
chained up in the yard.
You have kept your love for me
pressed between
pages of a well-loved book.

Secretly, with a diamond,
you have etched me into a glass pane,
showing me my hiding place
with a cupped hand.

I could teach the world to woo
but teach me to keep as you do.

In those days, before Theo knew about me, you took more risks. For that hour in the Empire, and for the two hours after that here at the house, in my bed while Sal was at school and Beth on site somewhere, you had to lie. Tell him you were staying after the botanical society sale to have lunch with a schoolfriend who happened to be holidaying in Cape Town.

I didn't take you straight to my room. I crave romance; I want to seduce you with words first. I love to see your pupils dilate, take more and more of me in as I tell you what you already know. That there is nobody like you, never has been, that you are the revelation of my life, my consolation and respite. That I feel safer now about striking out because I know that if I falter, I only have to

25

turn around to see your reassuring smile. That the year I met you was Year One. That moments before I met you for the first time, I knew I would fall in love with you, and consequently the slight creak of the floorboards as you approached sent me up into the high arc of a swing. I could have carried on, I did wax on, but then you reached across and said, 'Could we go now, back to your room?'

We have never kissed in public, barely leant against each other in company. But today I sat under the abstract canvas that has taken the place of the headless nude of which you did not approve, and the ghost of you brushed my wrist.

At a window table overlooking the beach, I saw a group of Holy Cross mothers. One of them, a psychologist called Angie, came over and asked after Beth. 'How long will your sister be away?' I heard her boots first. They are very spiky and resoundingly noisy. Beth once told me that Angie is a recovered anorexic who now jogs compulsively to stay slim. She must have some other shoes for jogging in, but I know her in jeans and spiky boots. She is slim and these new low-slung hipsters suit her. Her sexy bottom half doesn't quite match her severe top half, with its staring, slightly protruding eyes behind glasses. If I were one of her patients I'd feel like a mouse waiting for the wise owl to swoop. Angie's claws hovered briefly over me as she said if I need help with Sal I must just call. Then she was back off to her corner with a beating of carnivorous wings.

She must have reported back to the Holy Cross mothers because they immediately all swivelled round on their branch to stare at me. Probably pitying my incompetence in their field of expertise. While I was paying for my cappuccino, another of the group came up and said very shyly and softly that she wanted to organise a play. At first I thought she must be either a mad am-dram or a sotto voce pervert. But then she said, 'You know, for Sal to come and play with my daughter Harriet'. Harriet. Of course. Sal talks about her all the time. This was her mother, Hannelie.

Afterwards I stopped by the supermarket for groceries. No Coke, thank goodness, as Sal decided of her own accord to give that up several months ago. When you have to lug shopping up twenty-eight steps you don't want heavy, nutritionally irrelevant items.

I had a list and my foray went smoothly. I'm familiar with the essentials of how the house is run, though it's true that Beth has not relied on me. If she says, 'We need milk', or 'Pick up some ciabatta on the way home', then I complete the task. I was a bit nervous the first day she told me to 'buy electricity' but the staff at the 7-11 were very helpful.

After I'd unpacked the shopping, I came back here to work. Ryno's mother knocked and said her computer was playing up again and 'Beth usually sorts it out.' You remember Mrs Cloete, who lives in what was once a little holiday cottage at the back of our house? With a bad grace I followed her there and saw she had a game of solitaire going. She's seventy-six: I don't know what else I'd expect her to be doing with her computer.

So what's the problem, I asked her.

She said, 'It's clearly missing the jack of diamonds.'

I paused for a while before I asked, What does Beth do when this happens? 'She usually finds it,' said Mrs Cloete. I sat down and took over the game. The jack of diamonds stayed stubbornly uncovered. I clicked on New Game and the bugger popped up obligingly in the third row.

I have to go work now, I told her. I have a deadline.

She said, 'There's something I forgot to tell you. I'm always forgetting things these days. Ryno phoned from the Transkei. The line was very bad. But he says you must fetch Sir Nicholas from the kennels. They won't have him any more, they say his temperament is not suited to a solitary existence. He tried to dig himself out.'

So Ryno's dog has been expelled, I said. Where must I take him to?

'You'll have to bring him here,' said Mrs Cloete. 'You can make him a cosy little bed in the shed.'

Sal was delighted when she heard. You'd swear we'd bought her a new puppy and not just offered board and lodging to an old mutt. 'Let me sleep with him!' she said. 'I can wake up smelling of dog!'

I asked her, as a matter of interest, when she took a bath. Suddenly I couldn't remember Beth's routine, or if there'd been one.

'Rarely,' replied Sal, and grinned.

I've always marvelled at my niece's propensity for joy. She wakes up happy, exclaiming about something funny she read or saw the day before. She laughs a fat, full laugh at the nonsense she and her mother talk in bed at night, at her friends, teachers, dogs and cats of her acquaintance, everything. She's quiet sometimes, but a happy quiet, absorbed in long games and books, books, books. Other times she's less studious, gets on a pair of Beth's high heels and pushes a little pink pram around, pretending to chew gum and talk 'gam'. She worries about a naughty boy in her class called Noah. Last year she wrote him a letter promising him ten rand if he would just stop 'throughing paper balls at the teacher's back'.

At bedtime tonight she was less upbeat. I asked her

whether she'd finished her homework, and she listed all the tasks she'd completed. Then, 'There's just one more thing: I have to examine my conscience,' she said. She sat silently, bolt upright for a while. I sat next to her, as perplexed and wistful as only a lapsed Catholic can be.

I read to her. When I thought she was asleep, I started to creep away from the bed. I felt a steely grip on my arm. I understood that I should lie next to her until her breathing was deep and even, past the first light phase, the one that ends with an inexplicable shudder, or jerk; past the false start that precedes true dreaming.

All I could think about was how I really wanted to be on my own, reading my own book in my own bed. I have no gift for this. I've met nurturers before; never imagined I'd have to be one.

Monica used to complain that I never looked after her, never tucked her into bed when she was sick, never took her car to the mechanic when it needed fixing. How do I want to defend myself against these accusations? Firstly, Monica was always in charge, always announcing how things would be and then monitoring them so that they met with her blueprint. Secondly, I frankly don't remember her ever being sick. She was frighteningly robust. I was attracted to her strength, which seemed a good foil for my passivity.

My passivity, yes. As you get older, you grow accustomed to yourself. What I mean is that as a child, I kept expecting to turn into someone else – a rugby player, an academic achiever, someone who copes easily. It never occurred to me that I couldn't become those things, that they required internal and external qualities I didn't have. It took ages for me to cotton on that my interior life was in fact different from that of my friends. Only gradually did I apprehend that I was experiencing the world differently from other people.

Commonplace objects are for me like old books I have read before, and in which I have left a distinctive bookmark, an envelope, postcard, bill, ticket, shopping list, letter, or photograph that forever reminds me of the circumstances in which I first turned those pages. I move slowly through a world that is bookmarked with meaning. I can't get ahead, as other people do. The others have gone on ahead, are waving at me from their established careers, while I linger here, thinking about the broken handle of the handsome old Monarch fridge that once graced our kitchen. I feel there is something about that fridge and its absent handle that needs commemoration. The way the fridge only admitted those who knew the secret curved finger hook that opened its mechanism. I'm using the fridge as an example, you understand. I'm reluctant to instigate new experiences because I have a backlog of old fridges to process.

Poor Monica. Just as I, in our early cohabitation, thought I might still metamorphose into someone else, she too doubtless hoped I would change. Happy are those who fall in love at fifty, after all this fruitlessness.

Thursday 15th August
11.33 pm

Last night, when I did finally get to my own bed, a large mental doorstopper kept my sleep ajar, still linked to waking. The sound of the boats going out, the puk-puk-puk of their engines, is the theme tune of my insomnia.

I know you think of me. Often I feel and even rely on the warmth and steadiness of those thoughts. But I also suspect that I am not completely real to you; that you don't expect me to respond as a real person who is overpowered by jealousy and urgency. I wonder if, to you, I am a dream, ether-real.

I have been thinking about your mail last month where you said that Theo would probably be joining you when you come to the Kirstenbosch sales, when you go birdwatching up the coast, when you come to town to do your Christmas shopping. You used to do those things alone: we used to be able to see each other under the cover of those expeditions, however briefly. Now you say Theo will accompany you.

I wonder why you say that, write that, and then make no further comment. Because in effect what that letter says is, we may never, probably will never, see each other again, or certainly not 'see' as in 'touch' – however chastely. I receive the message, express my great regret. You reply, yes, you feel my sadness. Then it's over and we carry on chatting mindlessly – heartlessly – about our daily routines.

Or am I just slow to pick up a long-extant truth? This is what you meant last year, when you said, after Theo's discovery, that you had nothing to offer me unless I would join you in unrequited love. You were so remorseful. I thought that once Theo had stopped making you feel guilty, you would write again about an opportunity to meet. But you didn't; you haven't.

I think you never look forward, as I do, as a matter of course. You're happy when things turn out so that we see each other, but quite easily resigned to the other. It is this stupid optimist in me that is the problem. I think: I have this much of Theresa, this three-times-a-year thing, and the letters. It can't get less than this. And then it does. In fact, it could all go, letters, everything. And I wonder what it really means that Theo goes along with you now. Does it bring you closer, heal things, bring intimacy, trust, happiness? And if it does, you wouldn't let me know, not because you are deceitful, but because you believe that each relationship is completely separate, autonomous. And I will end up knowing less and less, understanding less and less. As Dylan says, *It's not dark yet, but it's getting there*. Though writing this, setting it down, has helped me to understand.

Today Sal asked me, 'Have you ever been into space, John?' I felt touched that she ranked her uncle among the astronauts. Would I keep something like that from you, I asked.

This exchange was after a day in which she played her first netball match, against the chop-fed giantesses of Laerskool Jan van Niekerk. Sal was supposed to be a reserve, along with the morbidly obese girl in their class, but they each got to play half a match as wing-attack when Harriet's nerves got the better of her and she decided to stay on the sidelines. Sal loved the newness of netball, the fact that her uncle 'lifted', the freshness of the day, the camaraderie, the bib saying WA, the eminent reportability of the event, the way her opponent said '*Kom hiersô*' and showed her where the drinks were after the match.

Angie stood on the sidelines in her castration-issue boots, bellowing encouragement at her twins, to no avail. Holy Cross lost 0-16. On the drive back, Sal cheered up the despondent shooter-defence. 'At least we went and showed them. We are Holy Cross Girls. We did what we had to do. Even though they've been practising for four years and we've only been practising for four hours.'

Monica phoned tonight, just as I was tipping the fish fingers onto brown paper to drain. She was in town and would I like to meet for a drink at her hotel and 'catch up'? I told her I was babysitting. 'Isn't that what teenagers do for pocket money?' she asked.

There is a James Thurber cartoon that aptly sums up my life with Monica: the little man coming home nervously to a house that is encircled in the arms of a monstrously overbearing house-wife. But the same way as you want to shake the little Thurber man and tell him, Get a life, so I was unformed, waiting for life to happen to me. And Monica was no housewife.

While Monica was out resolving conflicts between worker organisations and big corporations for increasingly impressive remuneration, I went steadily and unambitiously back and forth to my job at Karoo Books. One year when the company was failing or, rather, doing worse than usual, I even took a cut in salary. Monica never understood my attitude to money, that it wasn't important. If you think how all the luxuries I enjoyed those years in Johannesburg – meals out at restaurants, weekends in game reserves – were thanks to her job, you'll see how hypocritical I must have looked.

I met Monica when she was a student of my mother's. She was writing a thesis on gender in the South African workplace. As she was a graduate student, it was natural for her to stay for tea or drinks or supper after handing in a chapter. My mother and sister both being committed feminists, my father having lived off a tray and then died, I was in many ways the ideal partner for Monica. Because male sexual aggression was so strongly criticised in our house, and because I had been weakened by what happened to me in the eighties, my only hope was that a woman would make the first move on me. Which Monica did.

Her thesis was very well received, and she was offered work in Johannesburg. I wasn't doing much – some temporary shifts in the university library and packing books for a local publisher – so I went with her. I wasn't planning on being her longterm partner – I wasn't planning on anything at all. I had a vague idea that life began when one left home. Things still seemed pretty unreal to me, after the army stint and all that. I was lucky to find work, being so unambitious. At Karoo Books, as I say, I just plodded along, lost in my own thoughts.

My thoughts were mostly about words. I'd hear or read a new and unusual one, and it would occupy me for days. 'Segue', for example, gave a lot of pleasure.

Monica, on the other hand, lived in the cut and thrust. She was always being flown around the country, put up in top hotels. I'd fetch her from the airport and in between look up recipes to surprise her. She liked complicated food like roulades and terrines. You mustn't think I was an ace chef or anything. I was – am – just capable of following a method. And I no longer believe in roulades.

I'd try to tell Monica about my words – 'riparian', 'egregious' – but her vocabulary had been almost completely colonised by the jargon of ballparks, playing fields and nouns made verbs. We talked past each other, took no joy in one another's discoveries.

But she was appreciative of the food. 'Don't you want to be a TV chef?' she'd ask. 'I've got contacts I could use.' In Monica's world, you always acted for an advantage; you never did simple, homely things for local good. It only occurs to me now that my low-level gastronomy was a sublimated creative urge.

Although I always made a big fuss of Monica's home-comings, I secretly loved being left alone in the house. I never brought work stress home with me because even though Karoo Books hovered on the edge of bankruptcy through the entire time of my employ there, I knew I wouldn't starve or be homeless if it collapsed. I also didn't have to do housework, as we had a maid. So I'd come home to the quiet, clean house in the ominous silence that precedes a highveld thunderstorm, with a clutch of new or uncommon words – animadversion, atavistic, fizgig, recidivist, conurbation, rugose, sacerdotal, caryatid, wayzgoose – and I'd rejoice at my solitude. As night fell, I'd make myself something delicious like a toasted tomato sandwich or a bacon omelette and, without Monica peering inquisitively over my shoulder, I was able to begin work on what was to become *The Secret Life of Things*.

The Secret Life of Things was a series of poems about everyday objects and the arcane or clandestine stories they hold within themselves. The French clock with its tiny key Monica had inherited from her grandmother, a piece of driftwood I'd picked up on Noordhoek beach as a teenager, an antique Cape Dutch pestle and mortar Mrs Cloete gave me when I graduated, a bicycle bell from my childhood. All these things we did not use, or pray to, or even look at much, yet we kept them because they exerted a power over us. In the fading light I'd sit and stare at each one of them until, myself disappearing, they rendered their account. Those are my best moments, when the lines start to dictate themselves, and I become merely the amanuensis of thoughts that present themselves to me.

I remember a poem by the American Charles Wright, which ends with the lines:

> *I write poems to untie myself, to do penance and*
>   *disappear*
> *Through the upper right-hand corner of things, to*
>   *say grace.*

It's phrases like 'the upper right-hand corner of things' that we poets live for.

My life felt very small and private compared to Monica's large and public existence. She was quoted in newspapers, pictured coming out of high-level meetings in fetching suits bought for her by a professional dresser. Colleagues at Karoo Books jokingly referred to my salary cheque as 'pin money'.

It seemed less and less appropriate to tell Monica what I was thinking about or engaged in. She accepted with mild interest the few snippets of publishing industry gossip I was able to muster, heard my news from home as relayed in my sister's letters, and then offloaded about her own troubles. In Monica's version of events, she was always long-suffering, hard done by, conspired against, maligned, underrated, yet ultimately triumphant and vindicated.

My mother followed Monica's career in the press. She observed Monica's increasing bullishness. Eventually she told me that she had 'disfellowshipped' Monica from the feminist movement.

When I had about twenty-six poems, I approached the publishing director at Karoo Books for advice. Harry Botha-Reid was kind enough not to laugh out loud. He pointed out that publishing poetry was the most risky venture imaginable. 'Now if you'd brought me a nice solid textbook on business management, prescribed at five technical colleges, we would be talking,' he joked.

There were two or three tiny presses which put out poetry collections and I might try them, Harry said. He wrote the names for me: Tertium Quid, Cadmus, Finch. 'There's a whole art to naming publishing houses,' observed Harry dryly. 'But before you approach them, there are some questions I'd like you to consider. Do you ever buy volumes of local poetry? Do you subscribe to any of the little poetry magazines? Do you go to poetry readings?' I shook my head. 'Well, I suggest you start,' said Harry. 'You know what I'm saying?'

I knew what he was saying. That I hoped to plant myself in a literary scene that had painstakingly been feeding and tilling a little ground for itself. I put my twenty-six poems away in a drawer and started to haunt the poetry section of Exclusive Books in Hillbrow. I used my 'pin money' to buy new poets' work. I subscribed to *Thalia, Night Attack, Sub divo* and even an overseas journal, despite the exchange rate. I attended one public reading at Wits where they passed around a register, after which I happily found myself on the mailing list for poetry launches and the poetry circuit.

At poetry readings I was often bored, yet even the boredom was fascinating. I would sit quietly in small rooms while other introverts whispered their minute observations of lichen on rocks or droned in slow monotones imagined histories of shipwrecks they hadn't actually been present at themselves. I was engaged in a hopeless struggle to reach someone else's meaning. I couldn't seem to connect with the other poets on a simple, conversational level either. I'd stand in the foyer afterwards eating funny little cocktail sticks of cheddar cheese blocks and olives, sipping a glass of bad wine, hoping someone would talk to me.

Then one day at a bookshop reading in Berea, a poet from Cape Town was introduced, Red Moffat. His reading was natural. I mean, you didn't feel he had a special, portentous voice he reserved for poetry. His topics were immediate, funny, poignant. Best of all, his poems were short. I went up to him afterwards to tell him how marvellous I thought his poetry was. His sunburnt face and washed-out eyes made me homesick.

Red wasn't staying long in Johannesburg, but he took me to Soweto Stadium to hear Mzwakhe Mbuli. I was completely blown away. The man's voice was a double bass; his presence on stage – he must be well over six foot five – was utterly commanding. To stand there in a packed stadium and to hear the audience chanting the powerful refrains from memory was to return to the very origin of poetry. 'Who is in Lusaka?' he demanded to know. At that stage, who was north of the border, negotiating with the ANC, was practically everyone.

In poetry journals, in threes and fives I published all the poems in *The Secret Life of Things*, but I didn't show them to Monica till Finch Press accepted the collection. I had reworked almost all of them, mostly from a technical point of view. I thought that even if the poems didn't win praise, at least they wouldn't offend anyone.

I was wrong, of course. Monica read the volume from cover to cover and found it deeply offensive. She read every poem as a sly, veiled criticism of her, and of our life together, particularly 'Pestle and Mortar' which she claimed was an unabashed exposé of our sexual problems. All news to me. She said it didn't surprise her that the book contained not even the smallest love poem to her, nor a dedication, because she'd always suspected that I didn't love her. I was a weakling, a parasite. I just sat around and did nothing. I should wake up and smell the coffee. Get myself a life, 'pull finger'. She wasn't going to subsidise me any longer.

She was shouting at me, which was not in itself unusual, as she'd frequently lambasted me in the past for my inattentiveness to her long monologues about trade and industry, or for forgetting her dry-cleaning. What was unusual was that on this occasion I answered her back. Once I'd raised my voice, I felt quite exhilarated. So this was how bellicose people felt: the thrill of drowning out your opponent, pumping out abuse. When you're shouting, you open up a direct vein to all your repressed rancour. It is like being drunk but without losing the power of speech.

I told her that she was a grubbing materialist, a harpy who had betrayed the ideals of feminism by aping the grotesqueries of the male mafia. That she must be mad to think I'd write a love poem to someone who regularly and unblushingly called for the playing fields to be levelled, that I was happiest and always would be happiest when she was out of town.

After we'd said all there was to say, we were quite polite towards each other. In a mutually understood ellipsis, I started to pack my things. Monica even brought a cloth to dust off my suitcase which, unlike hers, hadn't been anywhere recently. The truths we'd just revealed had left us both as embarrassed as a post-one-night-stand couple. The near decade we'd spent together could be as easily erased as a film of dust on a piece of luggage. Suddenly I was awake, looking around our townhouse in utter surprise. Had I really lived here? Had I padded across these thickly carpeted floors to brush my teeth on those cold tiles more than three thousand times?

I moved into the spare room of a Karoo Books colleague, Martie Oliver. Her house was very messy and full of peculiar little dumb-waiter figurines in colonial dress who seemed always, solicitously, to be offering one a tray to put one's glass on, as well as some less tangible form of companionship. I found them kind and supportive.

Martie seemed genuinely touched by my 'Valediction to the Dumb Waiters' poem, with its refrain:

Goodbye, little men –
men of kindly acumen.

Monica didn't attend the launch of *The Secret Life of Things*. During Red's speech, a man stood just outside on the patio talking loudly into a cellphone about his planned camping trip in the Golden Gate National Park, as if he felt it necessary to remind me in this way of how unimportant I was. I wondered for a moment if Monica had sent him, but then came to the unflattering conclusion that Monica simply didn't care enough about me to be vindictive.

It's a mark of my naivety that I was completely unprepared for the bad review I got in one of the Sunday papers. 'Although ostensibly a study of the ornaments in his home, in *The Secret Life of Things* John Carson writes about the only thing he knows well: himself, himself, himself.'

I would have thought that one copy of the reflexive pronoun would have been enough. The reviewer had been at the launch. Her name was uneuphonious: Tizzy Clack. She described me as 'an incongruous figure in cowboy checks, looking furtively towards the door as if at any moment his favourite calf would come leaping in'. She went on: 'As the attention to detail in his poems is almost foppish, one could be forgiven for thinking this flannelled Carson before us was an imposter, a charlatan.' In her closing salvo, she said the collection might appeal to 'the sort of people who enjoy crossword puzzle clues that lead them triumphantly to obsolete words like "brumal".'

Lots of people saw the review and they all asked how I felt about it, as if perhaps I might have found it insightful and sartorially useful. It's true I wear checked shirts. I feel comfortable in them and I don't consider them worthy of comment.

The review left me indignant. After I'd read it, I went straight to Martie's loo and scrubbed it with Jik. Martie said, 'If only more writers responded to bad reviews like you do.'

As might have been predicted, Red Moffat found both the review and my response to it hilarious. He said Tizzy Clack was a twenty-three-year-old English Master's graduate who was looking to carve a journalistic niche for herself. 'It's not about you,' said Red. 'Never get lost in the illusion of centrality. It's about her.' Herself, herself, herself, I quipped. 'That's the spirit,' said Red.

Saturday 17th August
8.30 am

A soupy day down here at the coast, with a thick sea mist in which the smell of kelp is so strong you feel you are moving about in a cold bouillabaisse. Yesterday was a very full day so I'm writing this early to catch up on Friday's comings and goings.

I fetched Ryno's dog from the kennels. The absurdly named Sir Nicholas is a light brown labrador cross with speaking eyes. (Ryno went through a stage of knighting things: the dog's honorific was the only one that stuck.) Mrs Cloete gave Sir Nicholas an old cushion to make his first night in the shed more comfortable. When I went out to check on him this morning, I saw a snow dog, a cloud of little white feathers with two dark, soulful eyes looking expectantly at me. He must have ripped open the cushion in the night – probably thought it was what we wanted him to do, a strange custom of the establishment.

I told Mrs Cloete I'd take Sir Nicholas for a walk after dropping Sal at Holy Cross. The old woman said she'd just get her walking stick and then she'd join me. I feel I must be wearing a sign around my neck saying Please take over my life.

On these winter days, Kalk Bay is its old self, the one I remember as a child. Back in the seventies, many of the houses were closed up in the winter, or inhabited by mysterious recluses. The atmosphere of stately eccentricity was heightened by two asylums – Victorian honeymoon hotels gone to seed and leased by the state – and one private nursing home. Alzheimer's patients regularly escaped and collared me, or called to me from latticed balconies: Let me out, let me out. Perhaps these lunatic women had stayed here before as brides, I thought. There were no coffees, decor or antiques to be had in the Main Road, but two banks, a shoe shop, chemist, haberdasher, butcher, bakery, hairdresser, post office. A mountain stream, forced underground, briefly reappeared in the park, where we children would dam it and upset the council. Someone still kept chickens: you heard the rooster crow every morning. The pancake Kaya of today was then the station's newspaper kiosk, run by an Hellenic supporter we called Billy Bookstore. He was exceedingly grimy. Beth told me he once went to the False Bay Hospital to have some of his dirt surgically removed, but I didn't believe her. On the days of important soccer matches, Billy shouted, 'Hellenic, Hellenic, Hellenic.' On other days he was morosely silent, or incongruously sang a tune that went 'I'm in love with a gambling man'.

The bazaar which is now Hennie's Market was closing down its old departmental operation, where separate aisles sold pointed shoes with covered side buttons, Dutch remedies or fabric by the yard. I would stand in the toys aisle and already, at ten or eleven, recognised that the playthings being discounted were collector's items. More than a generation out of date, still in their vintage packaging. Never bought because you could get cheaper, newer plastic toys from the CNA in Fish Hoek, the wind-up rabbits with their tin drums and the miniature steam engines had an aesthetic appeal that made me want to own them.

Mrs Cloete said she remembered it too, old Kalk Bay. The ratepayers' association had been run by a man in a monocle who used to flirt with her. You were very beautiful, I said, and immediately regretted the 'were'.

On the beach I thought how once long Victorian skirts had swept the sand where I walked. I felt like striding out. 'Go on, don't let me hold you back with my snail's pace,' said Mrs Cloete. Relieved, I set out at a crack. I like to build up a rhythm when I walk. For a while, Sir Nicholas bounded along beside me. Then he seemed to have disappeared. I turned and looked back. Mrs Cloete had stopped about halfway along the beach and was perched on one of the low wooden fences at the dunes. Next to her, with a quietly protective and proprietorial air, sat the doleful labrador. At least one of us knows how to behave, he seemed to be saying.

On the way home, at Clovelly corner, I was dazzled by the morning sun, catching me right in the eyes. Then, just as we curved back into Kalk Bay, I saw how in the morning haze, sunlight had plated all the windows so that the whole village glinted back worshipfully at the blinding ball in the east.

I managed to get some work done yesterday afternoon because Sal went to play with her friend Harriet, leaving me with an uninterrupted working stretch. The first emailed submissions for *The Unofficial View* have arrived. I printed them and started sorting them into poets known to me and newcomers. Then I separated the newcomers into those that had clearly written and perhaps published before and those who appeared to be submitting poems for the first time. Very long poems – epics, cantos – I skimmed only briefly as the journal wouldn't publish them anyway. Experienced poets and in fact anyone who'd bothered to read the journal before making their submissions, would know this. I went through both batches looking for haikus and tankas and sonnets because nothing looks as nice as a short poem on a page. There were only two haikus, both by Red Moffat. Funny, quirky, eccentric. I marked them with a big pink tick and put them in a wire basket I'd marked Publish. I gathered the epics together in a pile and put them into an unmarked wire basket. I'm superstitious enough to want to avoid the word Reject in my immediate environment.

Then I sharpened some more coloured pencils. I'm trying hard to be scrupulously neutral, to have criteria that any poet, new or established, could meet. So I decided to work on a system of coloured ticks, methodically applied. I slipped the ten poems by Girisha Naidoo into my clipboard. She's highly thought of, but I personally find her endless troping on light, brilliance, luminescence, lambency and radiancy quite tedious, so much so that I want to say, okay woman, the universe glows for you – what else?

I put that voice of mine firmly out of the way and picked up a blue pencil for clarity of thought and purpose. Does the poet, however abstruse his/her imagery, know what he/she is trying to say? Interestingly, Girisha used the word 'clear' itself and all its synonyms – lucid, pellucid, translucent, limpid, crystalline – without necessarily convincing me of clarity. I went and made myself some tea, trying to work the problem out in my head. Is it because for me, everything is muddy, murky, dim, clouded, shady, that I reject her incandescent verse? And hadn't I, just this morning, noted the play of light with amazement? Concluding that yes, I was prejudiced, I went back and gave two of her poems a bold blue tick.

I phoned a builder and asked him to come and give us a quote for some basic repairs to the house. Then at about five I went to fetch Sal from Harriet's house in the Marina. The property runs right down to the vlei and the girls were just docking Harriet's canoe in at the jetty.

Harriet's mother came outside. 'Can I offer you tea or a glass of wine?' she asked. We sat on the stoep and drank wine from a beautiful stone decanter. Hannelie is a divorcee. She uses old saris for curtains and seems to make her clothes out of them too, but her ankles don't tinkle like an elf's cap, thank God. She talks in little Tourette-type bursts, with unexpected, idiosyncratic silences in between. Her hair is the type that can never be combed at all; it is bright red, almost maroon, and looks like it might burst into flames if brushed.

Hannelie spoke about her ex-husband, an SAA pilot. Driving home one day, almost at her front door, she saw his car parked outside another house in the Marina. All the houses there look the same: whitewashed, Mediterranean, with lush grassy verges, so she did a double take. Perhaps one or other of them had gone to the wrong address?

She slowed down. Then she saw her husband come out, accompanied by a woman in an apron, a toddler at her knees. They kissed like an old married couple. It turned out that he'd actually set up another ménage quite close by; in a house with an identical floor plan to their own. He was a happy, if unimaginative, bigamist. Afterwards another neighbour confessed she was aware of the pilot's co-marital set-up, but thought it must be a sect or something. Both women seemed so cheerful, she reported, she had even seen them nod at one another in the local café when they rushed in for bread or milk. Hannelie said she'd been under the impression that SAA had given her husband a punishing schedule; she had no idea that on many of her nights alone with Harriet, he wasn't up in the air but around the corner eating kebabs with his other wife.

As she spoke, Hannelie's eyes sometimes filled with tears, which rather alarmed me. I found myself willing her not to cry. Talking to her was like playing that fairground game when you have to use a steady hand to move a loop of wire along a live electrical circuit without setting off the alarm.

To change the topic to more stable ground, I asked her whether she was going to Angie the owl's party. Angie had phoned while I was editing to say she was having a few friends – 'mostly Holy Cross parents' – around for a fireside supper of soup on Saturday and we were welcome to bring our children. It was the wrong question to ask. Hannelie's eyes brimmed with tears again. 'Angie doesn't speak to me,' she said, 'because of the lice.'

Apparently, Angie accused Hannelie of not treating Harriet's lice and thus passing them on to her, Angie's, twins. Lice are endemic at schools, Hannelie tells me, and not even the most expensive treatments work. 'Because you can't actually put a really strong poison on someone's head. A woman in Polokwane killed her child by spraying his scalp with Doom.' Hannelie still had tears in her eyes but was now laughing.

Just thinking about nits, my head began to itch almost uncontrollably. I confided in Hannelie and she kindly examined me, even using a special lice comb, and said I was clear. It was nice feeling a woman's gentle hands moving across my head expertly. This is a primeval moment, I said, and Hannelie made a quick little primate face at me.

The girls announced that they were starving. I said I'd better take Sal back and feed her, but Hannelie said nonsense, she'd make them some curried chicken fillets. I'd never seen Sal eat anything more exotic than a chicken burger with garlic mayonnaise, but I kept quiet. Sal tucked in and pronounced the food delicious.

Hannelie and I had another glass of wine and spoke about Afrikaans poetry. She is of Afrikaans descent. You wouldn't know it, except that she pronounces 'washing' as 'wushing'. She brought out a commonplace-book, a thick scrapbook in which she has copied out or pasted extracts she likes. She read to me from Jan Celliers:

Dis al
Dis die blond,
Dis die blou:
dis die veld,
dis die lug;
en 'n voël draai bowe in eensame vlug –
dis al.

There is a second stanza, about an exile returning to find

a grave, shedding a tear, and once again, 'dis al'.

'I've always loved this poem,' said Hannelie, 'though it seems to say so little.' It says everything there is to say about being South African, I replied. 'No,' said Hannelie, 'I don't think it does really, it leaves out all the pain.' I said I thought the word 'exile' carried the pain.

It felt so good to be sitting there in the twilight, mildly disagreeing about a poem.

When Sal and I got home it was dark. Mrs Cloete was sitting at our dining room table playing patience with a Bicycle pack. Sir Nicholas was making sleep a transitive verb at her slippered feet. He was sleeping her feet, I felt, sleeping her felt feet.

I asked her had she locked herself out of her cottage. She said no, that the ace of hearts had gone missing from her computer and she thought she'd come in and play with our real pack which couldn't cheat. I said please feel free to take it with you.

The house was all warm from the anthracite heater I'd stoked up earlier. Neither Mrs Cloete nor Sir Nicholas seemed keen to go out into the cold night air, but I firmly walked her back to her door and switched on her lights and put on her kettle for her hot water bottle. Sal found its pink crocheted cover. The old lady was clutching it to herself when we said goodnight and closed her door for her. She looked very tiny, with her navy blue slacks hanging loosely from her waist, the fabric somehow snagged and balled with wear, and her childish shoulders stooped inside her cardigan.

I led the reluctant Sir Nicholas to his shed. Both he and Sal looked at me reproachfully. Sal said she thought I should make Sir Nicholas a hot water bottle too. I said look what happened to the cushion.

'Is Mrs Cloete anything to me?' asked Sal. 'Is she my other granny?'

I said, No, Mrs Cloete is the mother of my best friend Ryno. She's lived in the caretaker's cottage for years. It looks like she's a family member, but she actually pays rent. Mrs Cloete's family once owned the most fertile farms of the Western Cape, a long time ago, but now she rents in our yard. She still has some furniture and brass and stuff that is hundreds of years old.

Sal said she did think the crocheted hot water bottle cover looked old. I said there's an important difference between worthless old and valuable old.

At last I put Sal to bed. I fell asleep next to her. Waking in the middle of the night, I felt her warm back against my chest. There is such a taboo against this kind of thing that I dragged myself off to my own icy sheets. As I waited for them to warm up, I listened to the waves crash on the reef with the clarity of pistol shots.

Saturday 17th August
10.45 pm

If I had to imagine an ideal message from you, it would be like an advent calendar or rather, a web page with thousands of links, so that each word or phrase would lead to yet more words and phrases, sating my curiosity, answering all my questions. Click here to see what else was in Theresa's heart when she wrote that. Prise this little window open to see what she looked like when she said this. Instead, I find myself holding back, in deference to your privacy.

I wanted to send you a message on your cellphone about the two porcupine quills you left in the pocket of my corduroy jacket, but I didn't. I can't send you anything but these mails. You can send me things – and you do – but I may not send. That is why my words sometimes seem to be hammering at your door.

I put the jacket on earlier this evening for the first time in ages (Angie's party warranted a jacket) and felt something hard and sharp in the pocket. It was the quills. There was something I wanted to say to you about those quills.

I still have your number, though I know I may not use it. The effort involved in not doing so at that moment, remembering our walk on the mountainside and you threading the quills absentmindedly through your jersey as you told me my fate, felt almost heroic. I thought, those quills are weapons, but Theresa treats them like knitting needles, and gives them to me like pens. It started to come like fragments of a poem: 'grieve Theresa/ weave Theresa/ cleave Theresa.' Since I could not write it for you, I wrote it for myself.

Perhaps this kind of reticent silence is a good discipline, but I fear that once I start sending messages inwards rather than outwards, there will never seem to be a right moment to speak again. And eventually I will have a whole store of unsent love notes, about porcupine quills and remembered kisses and small sadnesses, with no foreseeable moment alone with you. This paragraph is not a complaint, or a suggestion, but a state of John.

I want to know about your life, every little detail, yet when you give me the little intimate dioramas I crave, I am caught by unexpected stabs of jealousy. One day you told me how Jackie and Liza were staying with you and you got up early and prepared fruit for them. You said,

'I peeled mangoes for Theo and the girls.' It took my breath away. Then I was filled with fury. Let Theo peel his own mangoes, my mind cried, let him eat them with the fucking peel on! The mangoes got me, they were too intimate. I nearly replied saying I'm sorry, that's it, I can't continue in the face of such betrayal.

Which is particularly strange, since being so close, knowing so much about each other, I even know that you and Theo make love every Saturday night. Well, Theo has sex, you make love. I even know how it happens, the sequence. How you carry on your usual conversation, started while washing the dishes after dinner. You talk about farmy things. I suppose you are careful not to stress that your side of the business – the flowers – keeps the whole enterprise afloat. The worldwide apple market has crashed; the Chinese, who have the original patent on apple tree cultivation anyway, have flooded the market with a cheap apple juice concentrate. So there you are, talking about the tunnels, the flowers and avoiding the Chinese. You make your way to bed, brush your teeth. Theo showers. You bath. In bed you lie perfectly still, reading your book. You never make the first move. You did once, in your early marriage, and Theo was repulsed; now quite frankly you wouldn't even have the impulse. Theo kisses you: once on the mouth, once on each breast. That's foreplay, apparently. Like a rugged traveller who packs only the barest necessities, Theo dispenses with mere caresses.

Afterwards he falls asleep quickly, while you go to the bathroom to clean yourself up. You use another bathroom so as not to disturb him with light or sounds of water.

Then comes the bit I like. You say that when you leave

the bathroom, you have to hold yourself back from continuing to walk, down the passage to the hooks where your car keys hang. Restrain yourself from taking them and going outside into the dark. Check your urge to get into your car and drive, pulling off the farm road onto the swishing N2. Then, since you are already on the plateau, you quickly reach the summit of the pass. At the picnic site where baboons and other muggers lie in wait for unwary trippers, you look down over the sudden, deep-below-you vista of the city and its seaboard lights, opening up in three dimensions like a brilliant set change. Then down, down you go, overtaking the heavy trucks that have been forewarned to engage their lowest gear. You reach the ugly low point of your journey at the dolorous traffic lights of the Strand/Somerset West interchange. There is a big electrical substation there that is the nadir of ugliness, the absolute end for everyone of every happy Overberg weekend. But not much further on is the left turn seawards to the old Swartklip road that skirts Khayelitsha. Casts of mournful chacma baboons and jaunty meerkats – garden ornaments – follow you with their painted eyes from the stalls on the roadside. A slight rise takes you gently round onto the sinister sand-swept coastal road – dense scrub to your right, high sandy cliffs and treacherous, deserted beaches to your left. And always, the lights of Simon's Town, St James, Muizenberg beckoning. For one long memorable stretch, surely unique in the world, road and beach merge; there is nothing between you and the waves. You are not a motorist, says the road, you are a gull. On windy summer days sand closes the road, or slows the traffic to a hot, frustrated caravan. On windy summer nights the sand drives at you in ghostly waves, making your heart catch with fear. But suddenly you emerge safely behind the dunes again, enter the Muizenberg circle, and glance across at Sunrise beach where once two lovers were attacked in the moonlight (she raped; his tongue severed). Once you have passed the solitary Herbert Baker mansion, you are within my ambit. After the putt-putt and the playground which in my childhood boasted a miniature railway and bumper boats with a dinky lighthouse, you dip beneath the Victorian railway bridge and join the gently twinkling old Main Road. I have memorised this road all the way up to Banderker's Superette (Gas and Convenience Store) in Retreat. The clock tower at Muizenberg station, though beautiful, does not tell the right time, but you know it's late because only one or two drunks linger outside the bars and restaurants, and the houses that rise straight up from the road – no two alike, a paper house from Japan next to a Venetian palazzo – are in darkness. Again the road hugs the coastline, but separated from its rocky edge by the railway line and catwalk. This is millionaires' mile: Rhodes, Schreiner, Bailey came here to take the salutary waters. Even TS Eliot once visited the St James tidal pool, where later my father taught me to swim by placing ten cents on the back wall. Perhaps the uptight poet changed in the gaily painted booths? The church where I had my first communion is on your right; and Holy Cross – stone-faced, deep and cloistered like the nunnery it once was.

But your business is not with God. At the blind corner you turn up the one-in-two gradient of Quarterdeck Road, my road, and right into its cul-de-sac. There is no parking in these narrow streets, but your vehicle takes the kerb in its stride. The path through the lych gate is soft and rich with humus. The steps are patched with concrete. The patches themselves are cracked. The outside light is on. If you came tonight, Ryno's dog would bark till I shushed him. I would open the door wide for you. You could come straight into my arms; words could bow out discreetly; we have spoken before.

That is why I can bear Saturday nights, that is why the peeling of a mango is worse than Saturday night. Because though you do say that you would rather be in my arms, you do not say, 'I would rather peel a mango for you'.

My poetic criterion for the day was the impact of closing lines. The pleasure we take in a sudden twist at the end of a poem – almost the same as that shocking denouement in good short stories – is probably inherited from our appreciation of the sonnet and its rhyming couplet. No, it's older than that, goes back even before Greek tragedy. I never read Frank Kermode's book *The Sense of an Ending*, but I like the title. The ending must carry the greatest weight, and do it weightlessly.

Dis al.

I chose a dark green crayon for closing lines, but even as I picked it out of the recycled jam tin, I had doubts about what I was doing. Isn't there something a little bit smarty-pants about the flourish in some last lines? You can forgive the Elizabethans, because they were playing with sincerity anyway, saying I love you, you're beautiful, I'll die without you, but if you don't agree to become my mistress, (a) you'll rot in your grave or (b) this [brilliant] poem will survive anyway or (c) I'll find someone else. Then the Romantics, who took sincerity more seriously, end on notes of axiomatic wisdom: 'If Winter comes, can Spring be far behind?' or muted hope: 'A sadder and a wiser man,/ He rose the morrow morn'; or silence and repose, even if imposed by act of will: 'Enough! Enough! it is enough for me/ To dream of thee!'

It was strange to read the sheaf of contributions, with

54

endings like 'The afternoon browned/ like an avocado' and even, 'Where is your father now?/ Your father and his cows?' against these noble echoes.

While I worked, Sal got on with her own life. I find that if she says she's bored, you only have to leave her to her own devices for five or ten minutes before she's wrapped up in another game.

About three o'clock the builder came to give me a quote for repairs. When he saw the old light switches and the exterior piping, he shook his head. The gutters and outside walls actually caused him to emit a long, low whistle. I can imagine what his quote will be. His name is Axel. I think that's a wonderful name for a builder, couldn't have picked a better one myself.

As I said, Sal and I went to Angie the owl's party tonight. Coming over Boyes Drive into Lakeside, the sky was pinky mauve – 'All dressed up like Hannelie,' said Sal – with a full moon. A ragged, low-lying mist lay over the vlei and stretched out to the flats.

The moment we arrived, the twins lassoed Sal with their arms and took her upstairs. They actually pick her up sometimes, and carry her, because she is so small.

Angie took me aside and said she thought she should warn me about Hannelie. 'Hannelie doesn't treat Harriet's nits,' she said. 'She passes them on like Typhoid Mary. I've tried to speak to her about it, but she takes it personally.'

I said I'd bought some rosemary oil and was keeping Sal's head fragrant and greasy against the onslaught of the little beasts. Which, I pointed out in Hannelie's defence, hop so rapidly from head to head it is impossible to find the ur-infector.

As I spoke, I felt again that compulsive urge to scratch

55

my head. I wanted to beg Angie to go through my scalp, with the point of her boot if necessary. But I knew she wouldn't understand my paranoia, would contort with disgust and recoil, wouldn't play the game like Hannelie. I gave my scalp a few furtive scratches and thought how interesting it is that every woman is wired completely differently.

There was an inner circle huddled around the fire, chatting. They didn't hail me or make room for me, which is actually standard practice at Cape Town parties. It's like there's this rule: you have to look at the other guests as if to say, Who the hell invited you? I found that there was a space for me in the chilly outer circle. I sat down uneasily among what seemed to be a group exclusively made up of single women. Angie came over with a glass of red wine for me. 'I see you've found the single women's support group. You're all lucky ladies because John is single and straight, I think, and quite domesticated.' Having dropped this clanger she departed to see about some snacks.

I found myself longing for Ryno and the low-dive, old-style men's bar he would take me to at the Klapmuts four-way stop. Ryno is actually quite scared of women, I think, despite his bluff demeanour. He went out for years with a girl called Sonja, the most dainty little creature you could imagine. Then one day, Sonja said she hoped he would understand but she was entering a celibate phase. Ryno was crushed. If she'd left him for someone else, he could understand, but the way she put it, he was not better than nothing.

After Sonja broke this to him, he came to me of course and we got quite maudlin on Jack Daniel's and Coke. Later the same night he used his old key to let himself into Sonja's place. She was lying very still in a buttoned-up nightie in her new single bed, her virginity completely returned. How do women do that, he asked me. Perched on the edge of this unfamiliar bed, the pine cracking against its bolts in protest, Ryno breathed toxic fumes all over Sonja. He cried and begged and generally humiliated himself. She listened to him for a while, then got up on her elbow: the idea was to reach across him for some tissues from the bedside table. Ryno mistook this elbow elevation as a come-on, so he gathered her tiny frame up in his arms, crushed her to his bosom and kissed her wetly (my detail, the rest is his story) all over her face like a happy dog. With her free hand, Sonja got hold of a glass of water and threw it in his face. That was when Ryno truly understood that Sonja was entering a celibate phase.

Perhaps that's why Ryno likes to sit at a bar in his leather jacket and drink until he is close friends with the barman and all the regulars. He is actually more emotional than most women, so it's safer for him to hang out with the blokes. Once we drank till about half past two in the morning when the Klapmuts hotel threw us out, but at least we had bonded. We were a whole lot of men milling on the pavement in the cold night air, swearing profoundly and falling down a bit. One of the guys said come, look at my new diesel bakkie. We staggered over, some of us with our arms round each other. While the others admired the vehicle, I peered inside the cab. There was a woman sitting there in a knitted hat, all hunched up in her jacket, staring straight ahead. She must have been there for hours. I called Ryno over to show him this outrage. Ryno roared with laughter. He laughed and laughed and said to the proud bakkie owner, 'Hey, bru, you check you forgot your cherry in the cab.' Afterwards I told Ryno how appalled I was. 'Don't be such a fucking poet,' said Ryno. 'Come join the real world every now and then.'

The women at Angie's party weren't the type to get left behind in cabs, though. One of them was dolled up in six-inch heels, with bouffant golden hair, a tight leather skirt and lots of make-up. She claimed to be a Holy Cross mom but I had her down for a porn star. As if for effect, she was sitting next to a resolutely dowdy woman who'd come to terms with her greying hair and her need to wear comfortable clothes. In the group, I recognised only the statuesque, sharp-tongued Vera, striking in a clinging black wool dress and her long dark brown hair in a thick plait. Vera has high cheekbones that provide an elegant shelf for her lidless almond eyes. She used to be married to Walter Kibler, the disgraced academic who was caught out for plagiarism. 'Other people's coat tails are Walter's favourite form of transport,' I heard her say once. Anyway, she did the introductions. Turns out they are all writing novels. My heart sank.

And what do you do, they asked. I edit a small poetry magazine, I explained, called *The Unofficial View*. It's not usually a paid job, but in this case the journal received a very handsome endowment from the estate of Hazel Feinstein. The idea is to give starving poets a two-year contract as editor, during which they are paid a monthly salary to produce the journal. It's not gruelling work, since *The Unofficial View* only comes out four times a year.

This news excited the women, who decided I was now the Cape Town publishing industry personified and moreover the epitome of a successful writer. They all seemed to believe that the mere fact of writing a novel would inevitably lead to its publication.

Which is not so far from the truth. No one buys poetry, or goes to non-musical theatre, or looks twice at short story collections. A novel, on the other hand, has a fighting chance of being published and, thereafter, of being read. Novels are literary bullies.

Stupidly, I expressed my misgivings. I said I thought you should only write a novel once you'd read 500 yourself. The porn queen started counting off the novels she'd read on her fingers.

'You've obviously read 500 novels yourself,' pointed out Vera, 'or you wouldn't have come up with that total. Is poetry a preparation for writing a novel? I mean, do you feel you'd like to write a novel one day?'

I told them how I'd once written the first 12 000 words of a novel, but then deleted everything extraneous and arrived at a good 22-line poem. I also told them what Red Moffat says about novelists. Red says readers should thank us poets because we cut to the chase. A novelist will say: 'He stopped by the wood that the O'Connor family had owned for generations, ever since the potato blight and the Irish diaspora.' A poet, as we know, just says: 'Whose woods these are I think I know.'

Because the novelist-women all seemed to be listening to me with amused interest, I carried on with licence. I said that when you invite a prose writer to dinner, they sit there quietly and steal your guests' best stories. They listen and listen and give nothing of themselves because it's all going into their next book and you can jolly well buy that if you want to know what they're thinking. But if you invite a poet to dinner, he'll pull poems out of you all like a magician's string of silk handkerchiefs, as cheekily as retrieving 50c from behind your ear.

Vera laughed. She said she'd been working for months on her characters' family histories, their blights and diasporas. Everyone turned to her. How was her novel coming on, they wanted to know. 'Oh, it's complete endometriosis,' said Vera. 'My ideas aren't pouring out, they've gone all retrograde. Flowing back inside me and building up malignantly.'

Porn Star had to have endometriosis defined for her. Once she had got it, it was open season on female complaints. I wanted to scream, 'But it's a metaphor! Let's leave it as a metaphor!' The women were feeling the pull of gravity though, they wanted to have this conversation. They were curious about the inner goings-on of one another's bodies.

I felt myself blushing to my roots. Of course being brought up by a woman who studied and taught womanhood, I do understand quite a lot about gynaecology, academically speaking. But Vera's metaphor had undermined me somehow. She's a conversational terrorist, I decided. I stood up and said I'd go get some more wine.

Vera,
I fear
her.

The men around the fire were talking about cannibalism. Lots and lots of recent, documented cases. I felt the whole room was obsessed with blood. I felt I didn't fit in anywhere. Sal peeped her head around the stairwell. 'Can we go now?' she asked, even though we'd barely been there an hour. I bundled her into her warm coat and using her tiredness as an excuse, we prepared to beat an unseemly retreat. We were at the front door when a woman came up and peered into Sal's face. 'Ooh, she's cute. How old is she? About five?' She's nine, I replied acidly. 'No, really,' pursued the nitwit woman, 'but she's so tiny! Look how my seven-year-old towers over her.'

Never make personal remarks, was the dictum my mother brought us up on. But not many other mothers, I assume from the offensive impertinence of most of the world.

It was comforting to compare notes with Sal afterwards. Sal said that upstairs in their room, the twins bragged about their high marks and then made all the girls pull up their T-shirts and compare tummies and midriffs. 'They said I'm plump,' said Sal, glumly. I told her she was gorgeous, that her soft skin and blonde curls were adorable. 'You are the sort of girl that gets painted.' Her eyes lit up.

I made us poached eggs on toast, since we hadn't stayed long enough to get any of Angie's soup. Watching her cut through the perfect, just firm, yellow centre, I said, You know, Sal, Angie told me you wouldn't eat the poached eggs she made you and the twins after school a few weeks ago. Sal looked at me with her round brown eyes: 'But I trust your poached eggs,' she said.

The poached eggs were enough for Sal, but I trawled through the cupboards looking for more food. I ate two slightly congealed fruit dainties which I prised from their corner of cellophane. They tasted quite nice and I felt emboldened. In a Tupperware I found a piece of marzipan with some fruit cake still clinging to it, which was quite delicious. 'That's enough now,' said Sal. 'I can't bear to watch you any longer. You're not a bin.'

What I was trying to say yesterday, about the quills, was that nothing has ever hurt me as much as your news that day last year hurt me. Until then I believed that you would leave Theo, come live with me and be my love. It was just a matter of weaning him off you, of logistics.

The truth is that while ending an eight-year marriage is like knocking down an old shed, breaking up a marriage of twenty years is more like dismantling an empire.

And so you came to visit me one day last winter. I thought it was a birthday gift, being able to see you on a Saturday. You said, 'Let's go for a walk on the mountain,' and I thought yes, and the moment we are in some secluded spot, or even just alone on the plateau, I will kiss her. We took the two flights of steep steps up to Boyes Drive in silence, and walked along the road to the beginning of the contour path. On the roadside, outside the gates of one of those dark, hillside mansions with absentee landlords, we found quills. Some clean, some with hunks of road-killed porcupine still attached.

Your mood was grave; anyone else would have seen the foreboding in your eyes. Still, I felt sure that at any moment you would be infected by the joy of our being together. I was happy, bounding along like a kitten about to be drowned or a porcupine snuffling about in the dark. On the contour path we spoke about the evidence of summer fires in the blackened vegetation around us. Then you broke my heart.

At the top, looking down on the bay, you stood threading those porcupine quills through your jersey and said quite simply: 'John, you must understand I have nothing to offer you. I have to tell you that Theo knows – Theo has found out. It's my fault, I must've made it so obvious, always rushing to my computer to check my mails, even going down to the office with a torch at night. And I made my phone give a special ring tone whenever you phoned. It was so obvious: I was so stupid, blinded with love. Theo will not give me a divorce. It's too expensive, and in any case he does not want it. He's been crying. Theo crying! I can't hurt him like this. Please forgive me for giving you the false impression that I could ever live with you, be your partner. In that first flush – I was so seduced – I would have broken down walls to be with you. But it's only fair to tell you that we cannot be together – that will never happen while Theo is alive. I have a responsibility to him. I believe in the marriage vows I took, not from a religious point of view, but as a contract. It's not a question of what I want or what I would like. If you are willing, if you will accept, what I can offer you, forever and ever, is a very painful unrequited love. You know, I'm sure you've thought about this, that the eight year age gap between us is not insignificant. Even if we could be together, I'd reach old age before you, and neither of us would like that. Look, compare our hands.'

You brought my hand up next to yours, which I kissed, and so you withdrew it again, saying, 'I cannot imagine what kind of woman will suit you, but I hope you will find her.'

You told me what I 'must understand': let me tell you what you have to understand. You are the woman. Having found you after so many years of solitariness, why do you think I would go ferreting for another, one whom even you acknowledge is beyond imagining? I will never accept this dismissal or the arrangement about

63

eternal unrequited love. Do you know how rare it is for two people to feel as close as we do, to recognise one another so fully? Are you aware that this page you are reading is utterly rare? That this trust that allows us to enter one another's minds is uncommon? I have known men who drive slowly around the block before going home, so intense is their aversion to their spouses. Tens of thousands of couples exist in a state of suspended dislike, secretly praying for release by death, the marital deus ex machina. I have encountered forty-year-old virgins who have never met anyone they could comfortably venture beyond the weather with conversationally. Yet, from the moment we started to talk, I knew we could keep opening more and more doors, keep moving through to more and deeper layers of understanding. I have loved you for three years and for most of that time celibately, though not, in my mind, chastely.

They say that the state of love is a biologically programmed eighteen months – enough time to woo, procreate and safely deliver a child. They say it takes two years to forget a lover's kiss, for the kiss to lose its power. I have outlived these petty benchmarks. I will live with this choice of yours, and by your rules, but I want you to remember that they are your rules, cruel rules.

That day on the mountain, with the rich scent of fynbos and wet charcoal, I tried to look inside your words for the Theresa I know, but there was no ardour there. You were stiff and formal that day because you were reading a script. Nothing really sank in, because I kept waiting for you to say something I recognised.

When we first came together, in our first days, then you were yourself. I will not listen to words that Theo has put into your mouth. I am waiting for the moment when your instinct for self-realisation overcomes your capacity for self-sacrifice. I am waiting for Theresa. I believe that she will come, perhaps in the second act.

I was up at 5.45 this morning, trying to work. Sir Nicholas was still asleep, not stirring in his shed. I confess that when I checked my emails, I hoped you might have had a wild rush of emotion in a sleepless night and sent me a little note to my computer via your cellphone, or from a remote internet café. There was a time, in our first week or so apart, when we'd write or phone at least twice a day, often more. Not now.

After seven, the old Anglican church bell tolls a reminder to the faithful. Soon afterwards you will hear cars rumbling over the cobbles, perhaps on their way to communion. You are not a believer, Theresa. I find that an anomaly. Because so much of what you do is loving your neighbour more than yourself. Yet you tell me that you believe only in our individual power to do right and alleviate suffering. And when we die? We become compost, you say.

What I miss is the dark, cool, incensed interior of the Catholic churches of my youth, the smell of old wood and the light, filtered through stained glass, glancing off the heads of the parishioners like God. The priests never said Good morning then, or asked us to shake hands or volunteer to bring a plate of eats to the next get-together. The litany was intoned and you stood up and knelt and sat down in turns, but barely conscious of your own movements. You drifted away, your soul could unburden itself of the endless body.

Sometimes the sermons would be about injustice or peace, though even in my altered state I found it hard to believe that God could stop the Nationalists. When priests started to hector us from the pulpit with propaganda about the Pill and abortion – always speaking as if these 'sins' were exclusively female – my mother said that's it, that's enough. We never went again.

Years later a friend invited me to hear a visiting priest from Belgium. Father Verhofstadt spoke in slightly accented English, each thought perfectly turned out and compassionate. He said a poor coloured woman with seven children had come to him in desperation. Father, I cannot afford another child, she said, but I am afraid I will be thrown out of the Church if I use contraception. He said, If you don't use contraception, I will throw you out of the Church. He was a good priest, but it was too late for me.

I'm looking out the window at the courtyard below. I notice that there is still laundry – Sal's tiny little school gym shorts and a few towels – left on the line from Saturday's wash. Nothing gets dry here in August; I'm going to have to give in and take our things to the professionals.

I've had this view since we moved into the house in 1973, when I was eight. Excluding my ten years with Monica, my two years in SADF hell, and the one year on your farm, I've looked out at those herb pots, at Mrs Cloete's ivy-covered cottage, the shed roof, the wedge-shaped coal store built into the corner against the shed. Right now there are some bags of bottles there plus an empty All-Bran box waiting for recycling. Tiny the bergie will probably collect the empties in exchange for a tip.

Above the washing line and the ivy roof, the blue sky meets the edge of the Silvermine reserve. When I was a child, small wild animals – baboons, porcupines, musk-rats, meerkats, guineafowl – used to find their way into our garden. But not so much any more, hardly ever now.

I've looked out at this scene every day for most of my life. But just today, everything – the towels, the gutter, the ivy – looks that much more composed, at peace. Like the Cape sparrows on the schoolroom windowsill during a Standard Five geography test, these objects and structures are impervious to one's private suffering. Suffering! How can I use a word like that, by what right?

I tried to read and sort poems. There was a wad of stuff by a guy called Vusi. I've seen him around at a few poetry readings, he's desperate to get published. As we all are. I once saw him perform at the open mike session at Off Moroka Café Africaine in Adderley Street. He's a knockout when he's extemporising. But on the page, his poems are all mad polemics or prolix historical reflections with ponderous or no rhythm, as if he were offering what he thought a poetry editor wanted. Written in longhand on lined paper, they are redolent with fake archaisms like 'o'er', 'yon' and the 'th' inflection: 'Tis true, the prophet writeth/ That in each fight there must one winner be.' Add to this overstatement, obscure allusions, puerile wordplay, mixed styles dating up to a century or two back, pointless inversions in word order.

It was as if he had successfully applied Langston Hughes' ten easy lessons on 'How to become a bad writer'. I composed a polite rejection letter, pointing out that if he were ever able to set down his performance poetry, I'd love to see it.

Sal interrupted me at seven. I led her downstairs and made her sweet tea and rusks on the faded Japanese bamboo tray. I fetched the Sunday paper in, and while Sal dipped her rusks, we chatted about the word puzzle and the comics in the paper.

The cartoon I liked depicted an attorney's office. Seated in the visitors' chairs were two figures from the nursery rhyme: the dish (sporting a fringe) and a very thin, perplexed spoon. The dish was explaining, The music, the moonlight, I think we just got carried away ... The attorney was drawing up an annulment contract between the dish and the spoon. It just got my funny bone. The spoon looked the way I felt when I realised my relationship with Monica was over: completely startled.

Sal didn't get it quite, though it set her thinking about couples. 'So you and Monica were like my mom and my dad, not really loveable?' I was as startled as the spoon all over again until I adjusted to her interpretation of the word 'loveable'. That's just it, I said, but we weren't actually married, and didn't have children, so it was easier.

I drove Sal to spend the rest of the day with her father in Newlands. He has another family now, two more children – an infant and a toddler. Sal quite likes playing nursemaid, and Ron's new wife Lilian is very bright with a textbook charm. As we came down Edinburgh Drive, we got caught in the left lane behind a small Mazda containing four nuns, while on the right a motorcycle rally roared by. 'It's definitely Sunday,' said Sal, and we both laughed.

Ron said he'd bring Sal back by suppertime. I had the day free. It felt weird, suddenly being able to do whatever I liked. I could go for a walk in Kirstenbosch, have lunch in a nice restaurant, see a movie, browse in a bookshop, visit friends – all of those things even. I was in a near panic of indecision. Is this how mothers feel when you give them a few hours off, I wondered.

I came home instead. Guilt overpowered me. Mrs

Feinstein's money is paid into my account every month and it feels as though I have done nothing at all this past week. So after making an ostrich mince lasagne for our supper, I washed up our breakfast things and last night's supper plates, smoothed the beds, restored some order to Sal's room, checked that she had a clean school uniform for Monday, found her stinky lunch box and fermenting cooldrink bottle and generally dealt with the surface of life before forcing myself to sit down with more bad poetry.

When I got this contract I was determined to give the journal a new edge, stupidly not realising that a poetry editor is only as good as his submissions. Although my responses to poems are usually immediate – a gut sense of 'good' or 'bad' – the title Editor has made me self-conscious. I scrutinise my own reasons for rejecting poems.

I feel fairly confident about my aversion to abstract nouns. 'Mystery', 'passion', 'beauty', 'peace' are words deserving of animadversion. You must demonstrate these intangibles to me, attach them to the concrete before I'll let you have the words themselves. As Ezra Pound said, 'Go in fear of abstraction', or William Carlos Williams: 'Not ideas but in things'.

But with other, evidently competent efforts, I doubt my own discernment. Am I rejecting this poem because it's the kind of thing I'd never write myself? And what have I got against the myopic, come-see-what-I-found-under-this-mossy-stone school of composition? Is it that resolute nature poets, the Mountain Club of poetry, refuse to invest themselves in their work, instead make it into an objective science? So that you want to ask, Sir, Madam, what were you yourself feeling at the time the kudu ruminated? Yet this school is an influential one, particularly in Cape Town. And to give them their due, they do work with that language which Pound described as 'austere, direct, free from emotional slither'.

I phoned Red Moffat. He's always very cool, very sixties. He once told me at a party that he was thinking of writing a book called *The Zen of Poetry Editing*. Red and his wife Frances were sitting in bed, fully clothed because of the cold. I could hear him relaying bits of our conversation to her. I told him about my nature poetry dilemma. 'You'd better represent the Mountain Club,' said Red. 'They can get nasty.' I said I was quite prepared to do so, but my critical faculties didn't stretch to sunsets and pine needles. In themselves, that is. The pine needle qua pine needle.

'Have some dagga,' said Red. 'Throw them down the stairs and take the ones that respond best to gravity.' I thanked him, told him how useful it was to have advisers like him in the senior ranks. Before I put down the phone, he asked me who I'd rejected. I told him about Vusi. 'That's a bad idea,' said Red. I asked him what he meant, but he backtracked and said perhaps it would be all right.

At the back of the kitchen cupboard I found a small origanum bottle with a tiny amount of weed still clinging to the bottom. I rolled a miniature joint and smoked it. Outside, a serious August rainstorm was in progress. The drains must have blocked quite quickly and water was starting to seep in under the back door. Sir Nicholas looked at me mournfully from the shed where I'd made him eat his lunch. I let him in and he shook his damp hair over me and licked my hands in gratitude. I dried him with an old beach towel, then rolled it up and wedged it against the door to stop the flood.

Feeling very different, I collected the nature poems and went through them methodically. At last I found myself responding to one about a tortoise and another, a kind of stream-of-consciousness meandering, about walking on Table Mountain in the rain. When I'd separated them from the others of their genre, I realised they were really quite good.

It occurred to me quite suddenly that perhaps that's what every poem needed: to be seen entirely on its own. I went to Sal's room and found some Prestik. Then I walked round the house pinning up poems at odd intervals, a bit like hanging an exhibition. With a clipboard in hand, I mused through the house slowly, stopping randomly to read. Quite enjoying the art exhibition ethos, I retrieved a packet of pink stars from Sal's desk. When I'd decided I liked a poem, I stuck a pink star on it.

That's what I was doing when Ron arrived back with Sal. Ron's nostrils caught a whiff of something in the house, but he's no forensic scientist and the dagga had embedded itself in wet dog, dried dog, wet towel, old house. 'Oh, cool,' said Sal, looking at my handiwork. 'Can I do this too?' Ron said he'd leave us to it.

As he was leaving, Tiny the bergie pitched. He said his arm was too sore to carry away the empties – a lady motorist hadn't seen him crossing the road – but he'd appreciate some cash to buy himself a drink. I estimate that I pay Tiny what amounts to a modest stipend each month. I stepped outside the front door, stood next to Tiny and stared up at the lintel. Tiny also looked up. It doesn't say 'Bank', I pointed out. Tiny's patience, waiting silently for me to complete my sarcastic antics, paid off of course. I found some change in my pocket.

Sal enjoyed the lasagne. 'After this I'm going to have

some more,' she announced, though when it came to it, she didn't. She said Ron's wife Lilian had given her salad and rye bread tasting of cobwebs for lunch.

It's interesting that you know what cobwebs taste like, I observed.

Sal ignored me. 'Lilian told me about calories,' she said. 'She said I should watch out because I'm so small I'll put on weight easily. She said it's cute to be a butterball when you're nine but not when you're nineteen. What's a butterball?'

You're not one, I said. You are so lovely I would kill for you. Lilian has a banal mind, I added bitchily. Sal found the dictionary on the kitchen counter near the phone. It's an integral part of our lives. With her finger to help her, she tracked the definition of 'banal' and its long line of synonyms. 'Yes,' said Sal at last. 'Lilian is banal. Nice and banal.'

Monday 19th August
10.30 pm

I could live without you, but it would be like a refugee, depleted.

I could live without Theresa,
but depleted,
a refugee.

If I published that, we would be quite safe. Theo doesn't read poetry. He reads non-fiction about the Antarctic, Everest, the Andes. There must be snow and difficulty or

72

he can't get to sleep. He does read fiction, but always the same three works, over and over again. *Moby Dick, The Good Soldier, The Red Badge of Courage.* The rest of English literature obviously didn't pass muster.

I remember when I first met Theo, he asked, casually like, as if the question weren't a loaded gun, what I thought of those three great works. When you've got an English Honours degree, people like to test you. I said I thought *The Good Soldier* was up there in the top ten, but the other two were – for me, personally – impenetrable. Theo gave a little snort and relegated me to base camp.

I don't want you to think I hate Theo. Wanting him dead is another thing altogether. I want to be with you, but Theo stands firmly in the way, as permanent as Herman Melville's reputation. Men like me, the sort that didn't excel at school sport but who aren't actually gay, have always been a problem to men like Theo. Their in-built sense of honour and fairness makes them stop and help us when our cars overheat or our washers need replacing. They help us as they help women. But then they see, at social occasions, how while they stand about the fire or the bar with the other *manne*, we make their wives laugh, and it puzzles them. They have doubts when their wives touch us lightly on the wrist in secret signs of intimacy, when their women catch our eyes in moments of shared understanding.

Theo would never be unfaithful to you. He would go into his workshop, place his hand on the anvil, and chop off his fingers before he touched another woman. But you came to me whole, unmaimed.

Twenty-four hours have passed, and I have loved you for twenty-four hours more.

Axel's quote came through on Beth's fax machine. *To:*

73

Replacing window frames and catches; Replacing rotten floorboards; Partial rewiring; Seal cracks exterior wall; Replace rusty gutters and damp proof, replaster water-damaged interior wall, clean and make good: R50 867.90.

Well, that's clearly out of the question.

Sal and I found it hard to get ourselves organised this morning. The weekend had thrown out our rhythm. Sal had to rush back into the house to brush her teeth; as we got out of the car I saw a tender little crust of toothpaste round her mouth and lips and repressed my instinct to use my own spit and finger to remove it.

Despite our flustered start, we were among the first to arrive at school, which is how Sal likes it. In the stuffy cloakroom with its detritus of mouldy lunch boxes and abandoned socks, I sat on a low bench while Sal showed me how she could just, within a hair's breadth, walk underneath the coat racks. I said please don't do that too quickly in future, or one night you might have grown an extra millimetre.

Then Sal unpacked her blue pencil bag from her blue backpack and said, 'Look how my pencil bag is camouflaged.' She knows I like it when she uses long words correctly. She has to leave her bag in the cloakroom and then trek with all her stuff up to the Grade 3 classroom. Jauntily, she put her cooldrink bottle in her inner blazer pocket. Then, with her nose just peering over the edge of her book pile, she checked with me that I would be waiting for her at the gates at 2.20. I kept waving till we lost sight of one another.

I think she has a right to her anxiety, though Angie says I shouldn't let her cling so. I keep meeting Angie at the pedestrian crossing outside school in the mornings. While we wait for the green man, and I shyly wave to

74

porn-star mom, Angie gives advice. Today it was, 'You and Beth are creating a dependency. I think it's because Sal's so short that you treat her as though she were much younger than she is.' I pointed out that Sal wasn't exactly eighteen and about to get a flat of her own. And privately I thought: Fuck off, Angie.

Our farewells, mine and Sal's, are from the shipboard (bunting, hankies, tooting horns) genre. Saying goodbye to Sal, sensing mothers around me doing the same, I realised: this is power. The power of loving and being loved so intensely that even if the flesh falls, the bond remains.

The sky has been dark and threatening, with cloudbursts again last night and thick mist on Saturday, so I allowed myself the luxury of a professional laundry service today.

Washing
As though casting shadows
rather than lifting them,
the sun rose
slowly, late,
like a broken heart,
(not now, not yet)
over the Fish Hoek
Laundrette.

When I dropped my bag, the woman said, 'Carson' and I nodded. There it was, my name, all real.

There was a dead penguin and a man with a metal detector on the gloomy beach. I felt sorrier for the penguin. Sir Nicholas rolled around in the penguin stench before I could stop him. The beach was wide and flat and it was icy, despite Weatherman Pete's prediction (low: 14).

I washed Sir Nicholas and left Mrs Cloete drying him off with an old towel while I did the shopping. When I came back and was unloading the car, I picked up a terrible smell of molten plastic. I raced into Mrs Cloete's cottage and found her quite obliviously heating a pan of milk on the front plate of her stove while three plastic ice cream lids did a Chernobyl on the back burner. She was very chastened and promised not to put flammable things on the stove top again or to switch two plates on when she only needs one.

After fire duty, I read all the pink-starred poems again. My thoughts were about first lines, how the really good ones stay with you forever.

Turning and turning in the widening gyre

About suffering they were never wrong, the old masters.

Batter my heart, three-personed God.

To condense so much, to bring plain words together with such breathtaking force. The simplicity is utterly deceptive. Behind it, driving it, are the hydraulics of feeling demanding expression, extracting it. I re-read each opening line with a lilac pencil, looking for hydraulics.

Of course, Theo's book list is also notable for its opening lines. 'Call me Ishmael' and 'This is the saddest story I have ever heard'. I'll give Theo that. Can't remember the opening line of *The Red Badge of Courage*. Does anyone?

At 2:20 I fetched Sal from school and we had our shipboard reunion. Will it always be the same? She came around the corner in her too-big school uniform (she will never be a large girl), with her laces undone and her fine hair in her face, a pile of books and a wooden curtain ring half wrapped in lilac wool, and I was struck again by the impossibility of it. How does she run her life? She reads these textbooks, and notes down her homework for Beth or me to decipher later ('LO test, grils bring PT stuff, sihgn:'), and chooses library books and knows why her technology teacher wants her to wrap lilac wool around a curtain ring – all these complex life skills – even though, in some parallel universe, I am still looking at her little scrunched up, wizened, newborn self through the neonatal glass.

When she saw me, her independence crumbled. I saw her turned-down mouth. I leant against the wall of the playground, came down to her level. She had complaints, fears, indignations. Harriet had put her 'on' in a game when she'd slipped and fallen and should have been given quarter. The twins had said that anybody who didn't have a 'Teen doll' was out of the group. Although I am outrageously partial, I entertain the faintest suspicion that she must give as good as she gets.

There was time for a quick snack before Sal had to get changed for ballet. The lesson is so short there's no point in driving back to Kalk Bay, so I sat in the Opel outside the Muizenberg Methodist church hall, listening to the John Maytham show and reading my book.

I was surprised to see Vera at my window. I'm always struck by her style. Today she wore a very tight maroon-coloured velvet top over a full skirt, a kind of slate-coloured silk. I thought I saw a scalloped lace petticoat peeping out above her retro boots. 'I'm a ballet mom, now,' she said. 'Alan's doing ballet.'

Good for him, I said. What does your ex think?

'I told him I had two words for him: "Billy Elliot",' said Vera. 'Walter's found another domicile, thank God. He can crash someone else's computer now.'

Looking outside now, I see that the All-Bran box is still there as well as an almost toppling pile of newspapers, lit up by the outside light. Most of the towels are still hanging wetly on the line. It occurs to me that I am not keeping house very well. I have been careless, leaving bread and crumbs out at night, resulting in a rat infestation which I have had to treat with poison. They have been getting quite brazen, chewing through plastic bags and lids to help themselves to sliced bread and peanuts.

I've noticed that these days when I give my address, people think it is very glamorous, the 'in' place. But there are still many families in Kalk Bay with dodgy wiring, rat holes (and rats) and unrenovated floors, walls and bathrooms. Hardly a week goes by without an agent or a buyer trying to prise us out with offers that run to millions. You can actually see the en suite bathrooms and electronic gates twinkling in their eyes. I leave their flyers and calling cards in the bottom of the post box until they form a thick damp pulpy sediment, not that the estate agents care.

Before she went to bed, Sal helped me bury a dead rat we found near the outside bin. She made an epitaph: Rat Grave. I said, I think you're supposed to say something nice or thoughtful. 'There was nothing nice about that rat,' said Sal.

Sal suggested that we let Sir Nicholas sleep inside because it is so cold, also to discourage him from digging up Rat Grave. I said it's true that he has an almost gothic attraction to the dead. Sal took this for a 'yes'. I thought what the hell, the house is already full of dog hair anyway. Maybe we should just silt down completely and when Beth gets back, give in to the agents and buy a new, clean house.

Dog hair, I notice, has its favourite spots in the house. The strands gently waft along tiled or wooden surfaces, amalgamating in a pre-arranged rendezvous at particular corners and table legs.

For supper I made big, thickly cut potato chips with their skin still on and Sal helped make a salad to go with them. Mrs Cloete came across the courtyard with a gift just after we'd eaten. A bunch of plastic hangers, the type they give you for free at shops. 'I've saved these for you. I always ask for them at Woolworths and Pick 'n Pay. One need never buy hangers.'

I knew her visit was not about hangers. She was lonely. I invited her in and put the kettle on, only slightly grinding my teeth as I did so.

When Mrs Cloete first came into my life, she was in her late forties, a very glamorous stage and later TV actress, soignée is the word, who could do both English and Afrikaans roles and play the beauty or the character. Ryno's father, also an actor, had just left her for a 'young boy', as Mrs Cloete used to put it, though I think Hugo Cloete's lover was in his twenties at least. Ryno was a boarder at school, and often came home with me for weekends. Although his mother was known to the public as Audrey Cloete and restaurant staff asked for her autograph, I knew her just as Mrs Cloete. The decision to let the cottage – usually only rented out to holiday-makers – was rapid. My parents needed the extra income; Mrs Cloete and her son were acceptable tenants. While his mother was filming, Ryno would move in with us.

Mrs Cloete stayed glamorous right through her sixties, and even into her early seventies. There were always men

– Mrs Cloete stepping into a late model car with a flick of silk and a waft of Chanel. But she regularly affirmed that she'd never marry again. 'I donated fifteen years of my life to Hugo,' she would say. 'I have no further plans for marital charity.'

In my mother's last days, she and Mrs Cloete would sit and read Simone de Beauvoir and Germaine Greer together, sipping sherry at wicked times like 12 noon. Mrs Cloete was pretending to be interested, or enjoying the role (imagining herself in a French movie with Simone Signoret), or maybe just humouring my dying mother. They were a touching sight. My own mother made no concession to beauty, never had, so with her, ageing was a case of growing to look more and more like herself: thoughtful, clever, compassionate. Mrs Cloete, on the other hand, put up a tremendous fight against the coming of the night. I thought she was going to make it – her hairdos were immortal. But then soon after my mother's death, about two years ago, she fell and broke her hip. Pain shook her about in its jaws and now she plays patience, collects hangers, gets anxious about small changes in her environment, hears 'Socrates' when I say 'cream teas', and likes to have her hot water bottle filled.

Mrs Cloete found the sheaf of poems I'd been looking through and started to read. Have you noticed how people like to read, find written evidence, when they visit you? Almost all my friends look through the pile of envelopes near the phone, checking to see who my correspondents are. I see you've got a letter from someone in Scotland, they say. Or, What is the Department of Education writing to you about? Postcards are considered entirely public. I swear they'd go upstairs and scroll through my in-box if they got half a chance.

'This one is good,' said Mrs Cloete, after peering

through her glasses for a long time. I came and looked over her shoulder. It was a poem about the Good Samaritan, imagining what his wife said when he got back home. I said I don't like religious poems, modern ones, that is. Mrs Cloete said she couldn't see any difference between the Good Samaritan and Odysseus. 'They're all just myths,' she said, 'a legitimate topic of poetry.' I read the Samaritan poem again. It was good. Another case of me being blinded by my prejudices.

To get Sal to sleep is not easy. First, there is the telephone call from Beth. I think this puts Sal on edge, reminds her of what she has been getting along without – her mother. Then there is the reading. Sal wants to read to herself, but doesn't want me to leave her till she's asleep. So I lie next to her and she reads her book while I read mine.

This evening it was a Barbara Kingsolver book of essays, *Small Wonder*. On the cover are two vividly coloured parrots, in flight against a backdrop of dark green foliage. Sal was envious. 'What's it about?' she asked. I told her the story of the first essay. It is set in Iran among a nomad tribe. A baby, a toddler only just walking, is lost, wanders off while in the care of a teenager. The tribe searches the hilly country for two days, refusing to give up hope. At last they hear a cry from the mouth of a cave. The baby is alive. But as their eyes become accustomed to the darkness of the cave, they see that he is in the fiercely protective arms of a she-bear.

Kingsolver leaves off the narrative – a true report, apparently, that came through the Reuters wires – and starts to track the abstract ideas of hope and the miraculous. Because the report did not mention the fate of the bear, this is left open. Kingsolver reflects, and chooses to believe that the nomads did not kill the bear.

Sal reflected too, following similar lines of thought, and came to the same conclusion. Personally, I think they killed the bear.

When I closed the book, she looked at its cover again and said, 'So it's true, adults get the best books.' And I knew that Sal's life would be ringed round by the great consolation of reading.

Do you ever say my name aloud, I wonder. I want you to, so very very much. Do you ever say 'John' and mean me, not one of the million others? Do you ever, in an empty room, give out my syllable? Do you confide in anyone about me?

After Theo found out, he was not angry with you, but with me. Desiring you, I should have chopped my fingers off. Instead, desiring you, I wooed you. Even before I met you, I knew there would be something between us.

The advert read: 'Single man wanted to help in flower export business. Free accommodation on farm. Would suit student or writer.' When the other applicants found out about the pre-dawn trips to the airport transporting buds, and the low salary, they withdrew. But I loved the cottage, and from the moment I met Theo, I knew his wife would need me. In his study, we established that I had majored in English, but was not a fan of *Moby Dick*. Maybe Theo liked my honesty, or maybe my admiration of Ford Madox Ford swung him, but he said I could have the job and the cottage if I wanted them.

I knew the flower business was yours, so I didn't anticipate I'd have much to do with your husband. He felt a kind of power over me, I sensed that, offering a thirty-four-year-old a job that we both knew was better suited to a young man just starting out. In his eyes, I was obviously feckless, hadn't got my career on track. But I felt power over Theo, too. I was the whole world of words outside *Moby Dick* and Antarctic literature. I was poetry, right brain, unpredictable, funny, a man confided in by women. When Theo said, 'Come and meet my wife Theresa,' I felt aroused. I didn't know that you would be beautiful, but I hankered after you even then. You laugh, but I swear to you that my pulse quickened.

At first you were firm, serious. You said that perhaps as a poet I would have romantic notions about flower-growing, but that I should know there was absolutely nothing romantic about it whatsoever. The industry was fiercely competitive, with the Israelis leading the field. The tunnels were made out of steel covered in plastic that had to fit with absolute precision because the slightest gap would allow wind in and result in expensive tearing. The roses were drip fed food directly into their roots, to avoid wastage. They were fooled into believing in a lifelong summer with blasts of artificially warm air; if propagation was required they were traumatised into the fearful state that results in new buds. When the buds were ready to go, we might have to get up in the middle of the night to catch them in their optimal state and transport them to buyers. Every day I'd have to walk through row upon row of roses, roses to the left of me and roses to the right, pierced by thorns so sharp they left the tiniest of punctures in the skin which, untreated, bred deadly infection.

I saw that you were fighting beauty and softness, that you feared them. Brisk facts were your armour; I could see you would not be quoting Gertrude Stein or Shakespeare, Browning or Burns. Poetry came back to me, but with a certain ponderousness at first:

> She is a rose herself; brusqueness is her thorn.
> Risking sharp rebuke, I'll gather her like corn.

Bad, bad.

I finally did the recycling today. The glass and paper bins are kept at the harbour and are maintained by an unreformed alcoholic called Cornelia, who sits in a ship's container surrounded by flattened-out cardboard boxes. She and Tiny the bergie have an on-again/off-again relationship.

This morning, Cornelia was helping a tall woman in a bright purple beanie chuck fistfuls of paper into the tip. When I joined them, I saw it was Vera-I-fear-her, and that she was distraught.

What is it, Vera, what's the matter, I asked.

'It wasn't anything you said,' said Vera, 'but I'm throwing my novel away.' She was crying like a child and pushing chapter after chapter through the mouth of the container. 'It's everything,' she continued, 'my whole fucking, stupid life. My car, my backyard, my ex-husband …'

I tried to stop Vera, but she's nearly as tall as me and no weakling. It was absurd, to be half wrestling outside a tip. Cornelia seemed to be on Vera's side, because she kept echoing her or making affirmative comments in Afrikaans. She was hoping for the slightest sign from Vera that my presence wasn't wanted; already I heard her

84

muttered oaths.

I said, Vera, I hope you have a backup copy of that, you really might regret it.

'Backup!' shrieked Vera, and Cornelia echoed her. 'I haven't even got a fucking computer any more!' 'Fucking computer,' repeated Cornelia with relish. Some passing fishermen looked at us with mild interest. 'And look at my car!' One of Vera's passenger windows had been smashed, and the broken glass lay inside on the seat.

I said, Cornelia, you watch our cars while I take Vera across the way for coffee. Cornelia nodded importantly. I imagine she watches soap operas like this down at the night shelter.

We had coffee and a cinnamon twist at the Olympia café and I heard the story. Vera's ex-husband Walter, temporarily homeless, had moved back in over the weekend and 'the fuckwit' had crashed her computer. Apparently nothing comes on when she presses the Power button, or just a tiny winking light, 'like a distant planet,' said Vera. She'd started working on her hard copy and found it 'execrable', hence the recycling. Her car, which she has to park outside at night, had been broken into twice, once on Friday, when the lock and ignition were 'graunched', and again last night, when the window was smashed. But she has such a high-tech immobiliser, all the thieves can do is damage the car in ways Vera's insurance won't pay for.

On Saturday night she dreamt that two black men, one young, one old, were circling her car. She assumed they were car thieves, so she challenged them. In her dream, Vera was a tiny woman. She ballooned into a huge size and loomed over the 'fuckwits'. 'Do you know how I feel?' she bellowed. 'Do you know how it feels to be a woman in South Africa?' The men were calm, unfazed.

85

The older man said, The problem is that you white people always think we want your stuff. The young man said, We don't want your car. Vera said the old man's face was heartbreaking, the face of an old family retainer. She deflated in size. The dream ended.

What do you think the dream was about, I asked.

'It's about me feeling small and powerless,' said Vera, stretching out her long legs.

And the backyard, I asked.

'The mountainside fell into it. I'd had a builder in, making gabions to keep the rocks back, but he hadn't finished. Last night I couldn't sleep because my garden gate, the one that leads up the back to the gabions, had unlatched itself and was banging in the wind. I didn't want to go out because of the cold and the rain, but at last I forced myself. I latched the gate and was just coming away when I heard this almighty rumbling. The rain had loosened the rocks, tolerance of error was overreached, and now I have a whole lot of the Silvermine reserve in my yard.'

You could have been killed, I said.

'I know,' said Vera. 'Dead under a rockfall with just my pink slippers sticking out. People are already starting to run out of sympathy for me. My bad luck is so unbelievable.'

At least you still have a copy of your novel on a stiffy disk, I said, remembering the party.

'I'd expunge that too if my computer weren't on the blink,' she said. 'It's utter crap.'

We laughed. I said I couldn't help her with the gabions, but I could get her onto Steve my computer boff and that I'd fetch Alan her son from school and bring him home with Sal so that she could get a chance to have the car window fixed.

After talking to her I felt exhilarated. Nothing she said was boring. She exaggerated and swore as a matter of course. Also, she used words and phrases that don't ordinarily come into conversation: 'expunge', 'graunch', 'gabions', 'tolerance of error', 'ballooned'.

At home, Tiny the bergie came knocking again, sending Sir Nicholas into a frenzy of barking. 'Is the old lady in?' Tiny asked. I asked him what he wanted from Mrs Cloete. He said she sometimes gave him half bottles of wine. This is the first I've heard of it. I suddenly felt furious with both of them.

I said, You live a very comfortable life, don't you? You can nap under a bush whenever you like, and no one disturbs you or comes knocking on your door begging because you fucking well don't have a door. Look at me – I'm supposed to be editing a poetry journal, trying to write my own, do the laundry, do the recycling, pick up the dog pooh, fill the sugar bowl, lug the shopping up the stairs, wash up endlessly, fetch children, feed them, supervise homework. And you, you just sleep in the park and hang out next to the bottle store, then when you're hungry or thirsty you come knocking on my door making my dog bark! I'm sick and tired of it.

I knew I was starting to sound like Bill Cosby doing parental exasperation. Tiny listened to me unconcernedly. Then he said if I was sure Mrs Cloete wasn't in, he'd come back later.

And knock, I said.

'Oh yes,' smiled Tiny. 'I'll knock.'

Nowadays, most people who are not like us have security gates with cameras trained onto intercoms. If Tiny could reach the intercom, which I doubt, he wouldn't be invited in, might not get any response at all. That's why the new breed of beggar loiters on pavements, waiting to accost people as they emerge from their cars. It's Darwinian.

Later I put some tomato soup to simmer on the stove while I did the ironing. I was wearing an apron and listening to the radio. I could see Sal and Alan playing on the sitting room floor. They had all Sal's Barbies and Action Men out. When Sal came to get them a drink from the fridge, I asked her whether she thought Alan was all right about playing Barbies. Like a seasoned actress, Sal looked me up and down, taking in the apron, the ironing board, the pot on the stove. Then, very dryly, she said, 'We don't have gender issues, John. Do you have gender issues?'

I took the folded piles of ironing upstairs and put them away. Passing my study I stopped in to check my emails. There was a long one from Beth. She said she'd phone Sal later, but she wanted to explain her situation to me. She'd fallen in love with her client, in fact they'd been in love all along. She wouldn't be returning on Friday as expected, but going on holiday to Mauritius with her boyfriend. It would be less unsettling for Sal this way, my sister thought, and also give her more time to consolidate her relationship with the man. If it worked out, she might move with Sal to Johannesburg. Then she was sorry but she'd need her share of our house, and that would probably mean selling as she was aware I had no capital.

What had got into her? It was too much to take in. Both being left with Sal and being separated from her seemed equally appalling. The thought of Sal at the mercy of such a wicked, materialistic stepfather. Me having to move out, find somewhere smaller, cheap enough, to stay. Which certainly wouldn't be in Kalk Bay. Losing this house in which I have invested my whole identity. Mrs

Cloete, Sir Nicholas, homeless too. I sloped through the house on automatic pilot. Everything was empty – the loo roll holder, the sugar bowl – I filled them, but not the emptiness inside.

Vera arrived with a bottle of wine. We had a glass together at the kitchen table as Sal said we weren't allowed to sit near them where we could hear what the dolls said.

I apologised to Vera for a smell I'd noticed earlier coming from the direction of the vegetable rack. Vera said it was probably a rotten potato. She started clearing out the rack, and found a rotten onion, two very bad potatoes and something that might once have been a tomato. 'Or a small ruby grapefruit,' said Vera. She washed all the surviving fruit in an antiseptic liquid, then scrubbed down the racks with Domestos. 'That should be all right for a while,' she said. 'Always follow your nose.'

I gave Vera a whispered outline of the Beth crisis before she took Alan home. I told her about my feelings of emptiness. Everything is empty, I said, even the empties are empty. Vera took the wine bottle with her when she went, saying she felt less empty than I did.

Sal asked what we'd been talking about. She'd seen the conspiratorial looks in her direction; heard her mother's name. I didn't tell Sal about the possibility of moving, just about Beth's holiday and the boyfriend. But with inexorable logic, Sal worked out the ramifications. She sat on a big armchair, very small and silent. Sir Nicholas, blessed with canine telepathy, went over and put his paw on her hand.

'Don't leave me tonight,' said Sal. 'Stay with me even when I've fallen asleep.' Her eyes filled with tears, brimmed like pools. Eventually tears started to run down her cheeks, but she made no actual crying sound.

I made ridiculous promises to cheer her up. That she could keep the dog; that her stepfather, if he arrived, would enrich her life in every possible way. I tried to remember the mogul, and found myself stroking the hardened lump on my thumb where I'd cut out a neat disc making his damn mackerel sandwiches, ten days and a lifetime ago. If Beth married that vortex of anti-matter, I'd protest at the altar rail.

I brought a mattress and put it on Sal's floor. When her breathing was steady and regular, I got off her bed and came here to write. I return now to my mattress.

Wednesday 21st August
9.45 pm

I did not sleep well. Even in deep sleep, Sal's hand reached out to touch my shoulder, making sure I stayed. I hadn't brought my own pillow, a loosely bagged amalgamation of foam chips that settles perfectly around my head, yet felt too lazy to get up and fetch it. Sal decided I was too far away down there on the floor so she joined me on the mattress. It was dusty near the floor and I soon felt allergens rampaging across my palate. I've noticed that I don't really sneeze any more. The sneeze mechanism has gone; everything goes straight to the tonsils, or rather the tonsil stumps.

In movies, children go to bed, just like that. 'You kids run on up to bed,' says the mother as she briefs the babysitter and puts lipstick on for the evening. In one movie I swear I saw the babysitter put the baby into its cot, awake. Then, as it lay down, its eyes closed like a doll.

These scenes are not realistic.

I keep coming up against the pictures I see in newspapers and magazines, in films. I feel as though I hit my head against these pictures, images of thin movie stars in impossible dresses stalking along red carpets; depictions of perfect interiors with bowls of decorative ostrich eggs and pristine surfaces. Life is not like this, I want to scream; it is cruel to suggest that it might be. It's only when the newspaper jokingly prints a photograph, taken from behind, of ordinary-shaped German women taking their traditional New Year's day freezing dip in the nude, that the public is briefly allowed to glimpse a natural backside. But then that's for a joke, a bit of a laugh.

My attempt to encapsulate this head banging feeling:

The media have failed me
I don't know how it is to be
an American when it snows;
how it is to cut red tomatoes
in a fitted kitchen, shiny clean;
or how it feels to see radiant
blonde queens come home
in photos in school magazines.

It's too much of a fragment. And I haven't managed to get in there my objection to the hinged dolly-eyed sleep of Hollywood babies.

The fact is that in real life, sleep is the site of some of the greatest battles of human will. Take last night. I stayed in the industrial areas of sleep. There you get pointless, wholesale dreams; you are separated from waking by the thinnest of partitions; you take your clock radio and the chink in the curtains with you.

The moment she felt my presence close by, Sal fell into a deep, satisfying sleep. She even snored a little. Meanwhile I kept wandering back in from these industrial warehouses of cheap and nasty sleep to check on my discomfort. Pins and needles; shooting pains down my hip; a stiff neck.

Sal wouldn't eat breakfast this morning. I listed eight different menu items I could make for her but she turned me down. Rusks, toast, cereal, porridge, French toast, eggs any way she liked them. A flat no. I thought she'd eat at school. I always pack her the kind of lunch box I would have liked as a child: naartjie, sandwich, nuts and raisins, carrot sticks, chocolate. In the afternoon the box came back with one bite out of the sandwich, one carrot stick consumed. She slumped in front of the TV, something she rarely does for entertainment. She seemed so unlike herself. On the one hand physically weak, but on the other possessed of a steely resolve to consume nothing.

I phoned Hannelie and then took a lethargic Sal over there to visit Harriet. When we arrived, Hannelie just happened to be frying a batch of pancakes. Harriet was sitting at the kitchen table, sprinkling cinnamon and sugar. 'Come on, Sal, I've had six already,' she said with gusto. Harriet, I've noticed, always counts her food. Sal hesitated, then something of her old self came back. She sat down next to her friend and tucked in. I could have kissed Hannelie.

We sat on the stoep with a glass of wine while the girls, replete, played in the canoe. They seemed to be dressed up as musketeers – I couldn't work out exactly what the game was, but they were fearless seafarers of another age.

Gradually, with the lapping water, the wintry afternoon

sun, and Hannelie's gentle, sporadic comments in response to my rambling monologue of woe, I calmed down. It felt so much better being able to talk about Sal. I said maybe it wasn't the news about her mother's delayed return, maybe it was the horrible little girls who compared flatness of tummies. I'd like to thrash them within an inch of their lives, I said. Beat them, as my mother would say, and unto death.

Hannelie did not seem to find my urge to beat mean children very surprising. 'Children can be nasty,' she agreed. But our eyes were on the happy game in progress at the water's edge.

Sal didn't eat supper but I think, I hope, that's because the pancakes filled her up. When Beth phoned, I thought of mentioning the food thing to her but then decided I wouldn't worry her unnecessarily.

I couldn't have managed this day alone. When things like this happen, you feel madness welling up inside you. Instead of proceeding logically, you flail and panic. Well, not you, me. It is true, I admit, that part of the reason I would love to live with you would be so that we could sometimes, if necessary, close ranks against adversity. That's what couples do: rely on each other and the third, stronger, person they make between them.

We are so trained to live apart, I wonder how it would be if we were allowed to live together? We could go back to how we were in the beginning, in our days of innocence. Those ridiculously early mornings in the tunnels with the roses or out in the orchards, walking the dogs with warm white puffs of breath in the freezing air. You giving me last-minute instructions as I reversed the packed Isuzu out of the shed and set off for the airport. Or afternoons in your office checking orders with you, printing invoices and sticky labels. I loved working with

93

you because I could read your mind, see what you wanted done next. In turn I marvelled at the way you could predict what the market would want or could sustain. Miniature arrangements: very vivid, tight, small bunches that could be put on the table immediately without any fuss, eliminating the problem of not being able to see one's guests over them. Rose bunches with buds so tight they would last the flight to Europe and still look just-picked. Your business thrived because you worked so hard, so meticulously.

In the rhythm of our work together, I discovered you. You are deeply practical, honourable, but also creative. You will work without stopping until a job is complete. Hard on yourself but compassionate towards your workers, the flower-pickers and packers. All women (except for one disabled man), because as you said, women work more neatly and with greater attention to detail. You started a little school for their children; you give them lifts to the clinic; you listen to their grievances. Not that they can manipulate you: you are quick to recognise a liar. From time to time I would see you telling off malingerers in a terrifyingly fluent Afrikaans.

I did not speak much at first, but watched and listened. And learnt. 'Now this,' you said one day, 'is red spider. It's a tiny mite which feeds off the greenness of the leaves, leaving them mottled yellow. And this,' you added, pointing to something that looked just like red spider, 'is its predator, Persimilis. Persimilis just loves to eat red spider. Right now red spider is winning, though, and we'll have to spray poison.'

I said perhaps we should buy Persimilis and seed the infected plants with it. You looked at me for the first time, I felt, properly. You went away to speak to Theo's farm manager, one of those nice, straightforward men who takes each suggestion on its merits rather than rushing to disparage. Yes, the farm manager thought that was a possibility. There was a man in Somerset West one could buy Persimilis from. It would certainly be cheaper and more natural than spraying.

I had stepped into your world, tried its language.

Gradually I started to realise that working was for you a way of avoiding being with Theo. Even though your business was demonstrably thriving, Theo would give you advice and criticism. He liked to begin sentences, 'What you need to do ...' or, of course, 'What you need to understand ...' We needed Theo to fix things, maintain structures and implements, but our best days were days when he seemed dispensable, when we managed on our own. Once there was a broken irrigation pipe. We both stared down at it, thinking the same thing: let's not get Theo in to fix this. Does he use some kind of duct tape for this, I asked. You said you'd get some. I trimmed the broken pipe and then brought the two ends together. You wound tape around the join. Your hands had to touch mine.

Then came the poems. Every day I would leave a poem on your desk: not one of mine, but one I thought you would like. This came about because you happened to say that you felt poetry was a gap in your life. You had loved it in primary school, but then some teacher killed it for you in high school. You'd never bought a poetry book in your life, but after I began to leave them on your desk, with a page book-marked, you would often pore over them, reading not just the one I'd singled out.

I did it once, spontaneously, and then it became a daily need. Sometimes I would spend hours in the evening looking through my books to find just the right

95

one. Each poem wove back into our conversation of the previous day. Since the conversation of the previous day was often linked to the poem of the previous day, we were twining a rope of interconnections.

We stayed near the surface of poems, but I remember the turning point. You had a friend whose very young child had died unexpectedly, after developing a fever during a day spent at the beach. You were fretting; all day you were on the phone, listening to your friend, speaking to other women, mobilising the support group.

The next day, I left an Irish poem, 'Child Burial' by Paula Meehan, for you to read. It starts, of course, with the coffin. You can't write about a child's death without that. It's the feeling produced by the tiny grave lying amidst the venerable lengths of dead adults in a cemetery. In the Irish poem, after describing the coffin, the mother tells how she chose the child's grave clothes – favourite clothes that smell of the little boy himself, and of woodsmoke. On top of his shirt and trousers, she puts a 'gansy'. The word isn't in my dictionary, yet you feel you know it. You can tell from the context it's a type of woollen garment. Do you remember how the word felt in the poem: soft and central to the poet's thought? Not forcing it, almost imperceptibly, the gansy becomes the meaning of the poem. She – the persona – speaks of wishing to wind back time, 'spin' it back. She wants to take the child back, not just into her womb, but before that, cancelling even 'the love feast/ the hot night of your making', taking him right back to a point where the ovum itself 'would spill from me into the earth/ drop by bright red drop'.

I was so filled up with the beauty of the word 'gansy', the brilliance of the spinning image, the fierceness yet softness of the tone, the driving desire to retract his corporeal being, the body that must be buried, so thinking what a fucking good poem it was, that your response took me by surprise. You were standing up at your desk when you read it, but you crumpled down into your chair, put your head on your arms and wept. At first I thought, that is the right reaction to a poem, to allow yourself to be a conduit. Don't analyse the damn thing, just let the poet's feelings rip through you. But then I realised from the sound of your crying that you had buried a very little son once, that perhaps you too had chosen his clothes, also thinking, 'It is/ so cold down in the dark.'

You said you didn't blame Theo. Little boys like tractors, you said; they love to be with their fathers. You said that though you didn't blame him, you simply couldn't be close to him any more.

On the scene, at the time, Theo was everything a man of action should be. Sent his manager to call the emergency services, tried to administer CPR. There was a ring of men around the boy. You felt as if you were being kept from your child, but that perhaps if you stood very still everything would be all right. Then you heard one of the emergency personnel cancel the helicopter. Not call the helicopter, cancel it. You knew what that meant. What you wanted to do was pick up the little body yourself. You wanted to wash him, clean the mud from his dear face, call him by his name, 'Joseph'. It worried you that his one wellington boot had fallen off. It worried you that a helicopter ride was something he would have loved.

In the months and years that followed, Theo blocked you off from grieving aloud, from saying things like, 'Today he would be ten.' Your husband did not want the mourning to continue; he set a stern example of dry-eyed fortitude. You just wanted to be allowed to cry sometimes, to keen like a mother from the Middle East.

Secretly, you observed Joseph's birthday; the anniversary of his death. You washed and kept his muddy toy rabbit, the talisman that he clutched for security, fell asleep with at night, snotted on when he was sad, had with him when he fell.

Sometimes you would see him when you were shopping. Standing in the co-op, you'd see Joseph racing naughtily down the tempting linoleum runway of the aisle, but of course it would turn out to be someone else's little blonde-haired boy in jeans.

You said you wondered in what dark, sealed-off place Theo kept his desolation. By contrast, your instinct was to speak. You even briefly joined a support group for bereaved parents. At the meeting you attended, you noticed that the room was full of women – there was only one man present. You asked the convenor about this. She told you it was always like this – fathers shut themselves off.

I'm not a hugger. At all the women's groups which met in our house when I was a boy, there was a lot of hugging. Afterwards I'd overhear the huggers saying snide things about one another. This has made me wary of the easy embrace – it smacks of Judas's kiss.

But on the day of the Irish poem, the day you brought out a smiling photograph of little Joseph for me to see, I made an exception. Perhaps I put too much into that embrace; perhaps you took too much from it. That was the point of no return, a pitch of intimacy from which we could not, and did not want to, turn back.

I think you thought I was intuitive, bringing you that poem. But I'm not. I'm the happy friend of coincidence.

Poets are meant to be comforters; we shouldn't fool ourselves that our role is any more exalted. It is not comforting to say, 'Don't cry.' The comforting poem is an open invitation to weep.

Do not think you will not bury
your face in his childish neck
again

Do not think you will not light upon
his expectant face
again

Do not think you will not encircle
his small, sturdy limbs
again

Do not think you will not read
his drowsy eyes to sleep
again

Do not think you will not hear
his croaky whisper, 'more',
again.

Thursday 22nd August
10.45 pm

Sal has decided to boycott all dairy products. I am getting very tense about what my next move should be.

After we'd dropped the children at school, Hannelie joined me for my morning walk on the beach. She suggested trying a reward system or buying low-fat yoghurt ice cream and things to tempt Sal without offending her principles. But Sal would scorn these strategies, I know.

After school, with blue shadows beneath her eyes, Sal refused a snack. I unpacked her untouched lunch. I said, Do you feel hungry and then stop yourself from eating?

She said, 'I don't want to feel fat, so I only eat when I'm starving.'

She is so very small, has so little spare flesh as it is, it wouldn't take long for her to become completely emaciated. My instinct is to keep talking to her, not lose contact with her even though her mind has moved into some alien territory I don't recognise.

I wish my mother were still alive.

When I returned briefly after my last stint in the military, my mother came to fetch me at the station. I'd held up pretty well, I thought. I'd got through, I'd stayed alive, had it easy by comparison with many. But as we pulled out of the parking lot, I saw Table Mountain, and hawkers in the sun. I almost cried. It was the sudden normality of it, I think, the sweet innocence of the civilian.

My mother glanced at me from the driver's seat: 'If you want to cry, just cry,' she said, 'just break down. I would.' It was the best thing she could have said, the opposite of: 'Pull yourself together.' We make the mistake, I think, of being too impatient for one another's recovery.

I'd signed up for national service against her will. She had already established all the channels I'd need to follow to be accepted as a political refugee in Amsterdam. I was naive, stupid. As a boy, I'd always admired the photograph of my father in World War II uniform, had romantic notions about being an officer and a gentleman. Also, Ryno – who hadn't deferred his call-up in order to study – was sending back swashbuckling reports of helicopter rides to remote deltas. He was in the media corps, documenting the war with his camera, getting special treatment. He said he'd eaten lobster one night with the officers in the last days of South West Africa, and afterwards they'd watched a porn film.

Beyond this, I was scared. Scared of going into exile, or of being imprisoned for objection.

I was completely unprepared for the army. Even the most vicious master at Boys' High operated according to a code of some kind. But in the camp, during basics, our corporal, 'Blikpiel', was manic. How he loved to torture. He scrutinised us, hoping to find a scuffed toecap or a patch of missed bristles on a chin so that he could vilify and punish. One morning his angry eye spotted a button undone on my shirt. 'Do you WANT this button?' 'Yes, Corporal!' 'Well, take it!' and he ripped it off and handed it to me – and then watched for the least flicker of opposition, hoping for escalation.

What kept us going was being able to mock him behind his back and occasionally, rarely, see him publicly shown up. Blikpiel's method was not unlike that of a crude stand-up comedian who asks people in the front row for personal details and then spends the rest of the evening making bad jokes at their expense.

One of the guys in our unit was a CAPAB ballet dancer. Blikpiel, who was so dumb his thoughts bubbled up slowly over his head in great, colourful, cartoonish pictograms that we could read at our leisure, obviously thought: ballet dancer = 'moffie' = weakling. So he made the guy run twice the distance the rest of us were doing, with a full kit on his back. I still remember our joy as this super-fit, ultra-strong dancer ran the route with ease, lapping many of us.

I survived the three months basics at the Infantry School in Oudtshoorn by honing my two greatest assets: a sense of humour and a way with words. The thing was to learn the language, not just the varkpanne, souties, bossies stuff, but the body language. Certain facial expressions could get you court-martialled. Impassivity was your only hope. If you stared with anything remotely approximating amazement, hatred, scorn, or even interest, you were treated to the deep crudity of the non-commissioned officer's mind:

Moenie vir my loer nie troep of ek ruk jou fokken kop van jou fokken skouers af en kak op jou fokken longe sodat jou fokken asem stink!

I memorised every insult and every outrage because in my free moments I was drawing up a satirical newspaper I'd called 'Kak off'. In spoof reporter style I described the goings-on in the camp. I had an advice column in which Blikpiel supposedly responded to real, heartfelt pleas for help with his usual brand of scatological abuse.

Dear Blikpiel
I am a new recruit and I am near breaking point. Please, I beg you, help me. Thanking you in advance.

Troepie!
Beter jou gat in rat kry, seun, of sal ek 'n koei se doos oor jou kop oortrek sodat 'n bul jou breins kan uitnaai.
Let Wel: Don't thank God: thank God you know me.

My right-hand man throughout this was a guy called Brock. He was very good-natured and accepted all kinds of rhyming appellations, sometimes just 'Sock' or 'Rock' but worse too. Brock laughed at my jokes, actually giggled till tears came to his eyes. He made me feel good. Brock also illustrated and distributed 'Kak off'. Reading matter was scarce, and time sat heavy, so we were able to trade the paper for food or beer or, in Brock's case, cigarettes. Brock was a bit plump, and another way he made me feel good about myself was that he was always slower than me when we ran. He was really scared of thunderstorms, and once or twice crept into my bed with me when the rumbling was really bad. I'd hold him like a child and he'd giggle. Brock giggled.

I've sat here looking at this paragraph, wondering whether I should try to explain that Brock wasn't gay, to my knowledge, or that I'm not gay, not bisexual even. But it's all so banal, these gender distinctions and taboos. What I want to say is that I held Brock and that Brock needed to be held.

He told me about his childhood. Brock's mother had run away with a man who didn't want to look after someone else's children. She was already separated from Brock's father then. One day she packed Brock's little suitcase and told him to stand on the kerb with his older brother and wait for their dad to come by. Brock was about four and a half; his brother was seven. They did what they were told, stood there on the grassy kerb until their dad pulled up in a Chev. Their mother went to live in Jeffreys Bay with her boyfriend. Maybe she intended to come back and visit them, but as it turned out she didn't. Brock and his brother were brought up by their alcoholic father. In those terrible Pretoria thunderstorms, Brock's brother would hold him as I did later. The boys tried everything to stop their old man from drinking himself into an early grave: spiked his drinks with aspirin to make them taste bitter; told him they loved him. But Mr Brock just kept at those brandies, as if it were a project he had to finish in a set time period.

At last, when Brock was doing his matric at Capricorn Park High and his brother was away in the army, he came home one afternoon and found his father haemorrhaging badly. He was dead on arrival at HF Verwoerd Hospital. Welfare made some kind of half-hearted attempt to put Brock in care, but he was nearly eighteen anyway and the Railways said he could stay on in the house for the year. He used his share of the life insurance money to do a graphic design course.

I met him on the first day at Oudtshoorn. An NCO was expressing a desire to rip off some poor troep's arm, insert it in his posterior, and eat him 'like a toffee apple'. I caught Brock's eye; his eyebrows just slightly raised, showing that willingness to be amused that all my best friends have had. He didn't look the type to survive basics. There was a softness to him, not just of the flesh, and as I say, his eyes smiled. He did not look *paraat*. Well, he surprised us all. The only thing he couldn't handle was his rifle. No matter how many times he was adjured to look after it like his wife, it was always dirty and frequently jammed. He shut his eyes during target practice.

Apart from Brock, the other thing that lightened my long days in the Little Karoo was being put in charge of the literary education of the RSM's daughters. Henrietta was fourteen and Lana was sixteen, and they were struggling with *A Midsummer Night's Dream* and *Lord of the Flies* respectively. I liked these nubile girls very much. They had lovely straight teeth set in voluptuous lips and the gazelle-like legs of track athletes. Indeed, they frequently attended our tutorials in hockey skirts or tennis dresses. They loved to laugh at me as I acted out their setworks or paraphrased them in very earthy Afrikaans. I wasn't such a fool as to come on to Henrietta or the siren, Lana, but I did flirt with their more full-blown rose of a mother. Mrs Viljoen was always slightly breathless, kicking off her high heels after a ladies' luncheon or a big shop, plopping into a large floral armchair with her legs disconcertingly apart – her skirt slipping between her thighs – and fanning herself with what looked like important military documents. I remember her painted toenails as she eased her stockinged feet against the thick pile carpet. I could endure parade ground suffering, knowing that my week would end in their cool dark dining room, with books spread about on the French-polished table, with milk tart and china cups on a tray, with tanned legs brought briefly to a standstill.

Our training consisted of running around with telephone poles on our shoulders, and fetching leaves (they were always the wrong leaves) from distant *haak-en-steek* trees. Brock's puppy fat fell away quite dramatically. As a result of this strenuous exercise, at the end of basics we were both classified G1K1. It was not a good time to be declared fit, when G1K1s were being sent to the border or into the townships.

We were given a pass after basics; we could go home. Back in Kalk Bay, I kept drinking as heavily as we had in our barracks. I fell unconscious one night in the bathroom. Luckily I hadn't locked the door. My mother came in and tried to help me get up. I asked her for name, rank and number and wouldn't get up till she had supplied them.

In this three-week period I slept with more than one of Beth's friends. Don't remember their names or faces. I'm not, as they say, proud of it. They were the kind of women who treat sex as the natural sequel to an afternoon on the mountain or in the pub. No big deal, and I was happy enough to round off their days for them. After all, I hadn't had sex since a brief affair with one of my lecturers when I was an Honours student. I went in to fetch an essay late one afternoon. Not long afterwards the door was locked and we were on the desk. We'd keep meeting in ridiculous, cramped circumstances, like in her car. Again, I was very willing. Still, I wondered what it would be like for me to do the seducing – for me to feel that strongly.

Back at camp, I had a lucky break. It was Mrs Viljoen who suggested to her husband that I be given the task of running the base's tuck shop. The tuck shop at Oudtshoorn – and at every other base nationwide – had been robbed blind by a succession of corporals who treated them as private fiefdoms to be looted. It was our RSM's fervent wish to show his superiors in Pretoria that he at least ran a tight ship. He agreed with his wife's assessment of my morality. If I could be trusted every Saturday morning not to ravish his two lilies, I could be trusted with the peppermint crisps and the petty cash.

So began the most pleasant part of my national service. I think I can honestly say that I loved that tuck shop. It was not a thing of beauty – a concrete cube that had perhaps once been an ammunition store – but it was my refuge. Mrs Viljoen taught me double-entry bookkeeping, Mars Bars bought and Mars Bars sold. She called me 'skat'. Apart from chocolates, we also sold pies and hot dogs. Once a week we went into town and bought viennas in bulk; a sinister-looking van from some Brave New World-type factory outlet delivered the pies. A high counter kept thieving hands at bay, and we flurried about in the small space behind it, warming pies and scalding viennas as if our lives depended upon it. Afterwards Mrs

Viljoen would have to fan herself a lot and talk very breathlessly, like someone who has come through an unnerving experience.

In the first week of tuck shop heaven, I spared a thought for Brock. There was movement in the camp, something was going on. There were rumours about a battalion being sent to Rundu. I asked Mrs Viljoen if Brock couldn't join us, come work at the shop. Mrs Viljoen laughed very prettily and said she didn't think so, her husband didn't like Jews. 'They even circumcise their names, you know. Brock was most likely Brockowitz,' she said.

I was puzzled because Brock had never mentioned any Shabbat dinners. His family was far too dysfunctional to be Jewish. Up to this point I had liked the Viljoens, even the RSM himself, fooled myself perhaps into thinking we had a lot in common. I saw Brock leave the camp on the back of a big truck.

If I thought I was going to be allowed to carry on selling confectionery while the country's borders went up in flames, I was mistaken. I was posted to a clerical position at Voortrekkerhoogte in Pretoria. Suddenly, there was very little to do. There is no boredom like that kind of boredom. Perhaps once or twice a week a file would land on my desk; perhaps once or twice a week I would have to deliver a file by hand to an officer in another building. Beyond that, nothing. Nothing, but not leisure. I was not allowed to sleep or read or leave my post. I had to be awake and alert, but doing nothing.

My desk faced the wall, at which I stared. In the course of my in-depth observation of it, I realised that the wall was two-tone: the wainscot a slightly darker shade of beige than the prefabricated surface above it. There were no other pictures or objects to look at, so I had plenty of time to reflect upon the nature of beige. There were three tiny marks, minuscule black spots, on the paler beige. If I stared at them till my eyes nearly blurred, the spots would assume anthropomorphic shapes.

I also counted. I counted the number of times the phone rang in adjoining offices, or the number of people who walked behind me. (I was in a kind of passageway outside the captain's office.) I would only allow myself to look at my watch once the phone had rung five times. Some mornings it did not ring at all. I calculated the number of Fridays or Tuesdays or lunches I still had left. I'd get confused and have to start again. The calendar in my mind looked like a child's board game, little daily squares to move one's counter along.

One morning a file arrived on my desk. All files were marked 'Urgent' or 'Confidential' or both, so it was not these labels that aroused my curiosity in particular, though this one also had 'Classified' stamped on it. I always opened the files because even though they were nothing to do with me (my job was to pass them on), they were at least something to divert my mind. The files contained details of funerals. My captain processed the funerals of boys who accidentally killed themselves while cleaning their guns or misusing army vehicles.

The file I opened was heavier than usual, and secured with an elastic band. It was Brock's. A paper-clipped note mentioned the need to trace his mother and brother. The documents said he had been cleaning his gun when a bullet, jammed in the barrel, suddenly released itself. The file was so bulky because it also contained a small diary found in Brock's possession.

I had to read fast. *Swamp water, flies, rat packs, FAPLA, rocket fire, shonas.* So Brock had been in Angola.

108

He was no good at cleaning his gun, that was true, but still – he had died in action, not by accident. The diary confirmed this. It was a small bound book, but there was one loose leaf tucked in the middle. I extracted it and slipped it into my pocket before snapping the elastic band back around the file and taking it to the captain. Later I unfolded the paper in private. This is what he'd written:

Cuito Cuanavale on the Cuanavale river
Cuito Cuanavale
on the Cuanavale river

The trench I am digging
to hide my bones
contains bones already –
the bones of my enemy
still dressed to meet me.

I am wearing my enemy's watch,
I am eating my enemy's tuna –
Why not hide in my enemy's grave?

I went to Brock's funeral: it was a hurried burial in the cemetery to the west of the city centre. But there were more people there than I'd expected: his mother with a drawn-on face, two friends from school, an old neighbour, someone who'd taught him design at the technical college, and his brother. I introduced myself and then steeled myself to ask, had he seen the body? He had seen the bag, he said, but had been instructed not to open it. I thought he wasn't going to say any more, but then he said, 'I felt his outline through the bag. It was him.'

To delay my return to the base, I caught a bus to the Brooklyn library after the ceremony and looked up

'Brock' in a book on surnames. 'Old English for badger', it said; and 'Old French for young stag'. The third option was 'Dweller by the brook or by the water-meadow'. Yes, that was him: burrowing, rustic, nervous, hunted. Belonging to some more ancient yeoman past, out of place in the savannah, a long way from home. I looked up my own name. 'Dweller by the marsh', it said, 'son of Carra (spear)'.

At last I was given my *uitklaar* papers. The captain said someone must have pulled strings on my behalf, because I wasn't being called up for any more camps. 'I hear you turned that tuck shop around,' he said. But the truth was, camps were being phased out. I went home.

My mother let me lie in bed, didn't cross-question me about what my plans for the future might be. I listened to the quiet noises around the house – doors opening, brief conversations, taps being switched on and pots of water filled for cooking, the sound of onions sizzling in the pan, or a distant radio. I was restored by the rhythm of life.

I got up at last. My mother found me a pleasantly dull thesis on management styles in the City Council to edit.

There are times when we have to be carried.

If I take Sal to Beth's GP he will talk down to her. Though it might help for him to weigh her, show her where she is on the chart and point out that she won't grow tall if her body is starved. I feel that Sal is watching me, checking to see what I'm going to do.

Usually when she comes home, Sal eats and then starts playing immediately. Usually, she knows exactly what her next game will be. But today she curled up on her bed and lay there, dully. Hunger pains were stabbing her. She knew that on the kitchen table was a fresh Portuguese loaf, her favourite. But she was conquering appetite.

I am trying to work this out in my head, trying to trace how it started, find the first cause. Beth has been a weight-watcher in her time, but not obsessively so. Still, Sal has noticed low-fat this and diet that. Mrs Cloete once regaled us all, in Sal's presence, with stories of keeping her figure in her heyday on the stage by sucking all day on a sponge filled with water or eating only boiled eggs and tomatoes for three days.

Then there is the great droning on about thinness in the media – not that Sal is a TV watcher, but she does play with other little girls who've imbibed the message that thin is the new holy. Sal is small, still has the roundedness of a younger child, whereas her friends are elongating, becoming coltish. So all of these factors are present. But I've read and heard enough about the topic to know that excessive dieting goes beyond the level of mere image.

I remember you told me once how you were taken shopping for clothes by your mother as a child. A trip to the big city of East London. You looked in the usual shops, the family stores with their different departments, but then persuaded your mother to take you into a fashionable children's boutique. There was a man in the shop – you're not sure whether he was the owner or a talent scout or a fashion designer – but he looked at you and said, 'If you lost three pounds, you could be a model.' Your mother was furious, whipped you out of the shop immediately. You said that you felt embarrassed, as if someone had told you to move up, you were taking up too much room. You tell me that at last now, in your mid-forties, you're happy with the way you look. 'I'm reconciled to my hips,' you said, and I said, I am devoted to them.

I tried to concentrate on poetry editing for a while today,

111

but it seems so irrelevant next to the crisis I am facing. It occurred to me that Sal might need me to give her permission to eat, since she wouldn't give it to herself. So I said, I'm going downstairs now to cut you a piece of bread and make us both some tea. I was pouring boiling water onto our tea-bags when I heard her footsteps on the stairs. She ate the bread. Strategically, I didn't offer her another slice, or ask her if she'd like anything on it. It felt absolutely delicate. She drained her teacup. Milk and sugar, I thought, thank God for that.

Afterwards I helped her with her homework. The scrap of food had revived her, and she responded eagerly to the idea of taking the dog for a walk. I sent her to ask Mrs Cloete if she'd like to come along, and the three – four – of us had our constitutional among the gnarled Port Jackson at the vlei in Muizenberg. Mrs Cloete made us laugh by saying she thinks she must be ready to die because she is starting to look forward to seeing Hugo – her gay, deceased ex-husband – again.

I cooked pork bangers for our supper. Though she wouldn't touch the mashed potato (I do like to make it with a lot of butter), Sal was happy to eat a sausage. Again I made no particular comment about it. We found a programme about dogs to watch on TV, and Sir Nicholas obliged by cocking an ear at the sound of puppies barking. Sal fell asleep without reading. I tiptoed in an hour ago and saw her lying sprawled across her bed with the air of one who richly deserves this rest.

I've finished reading the Barbara Kingsolver book. I think it's very good – she's an excellent writer. But there's something slightly smug in her attitude or tone that grates me slightly, for example feeling so proud about bringing her children up so well, without a TV set or Barbies, for having just the right thought for every occasion. What about just being wrong sometimes? Madly, hilariously wrong?

What shall I read next? What are you reading?

How I think of you. I ponder everything you have said, and even some of the things you don't say. Today I remembered exactly a moment when you used the word 'attrition'. It was in 2000, the year my mother was dying. We were coming out of the bank in Grabouw where we'd gone to draw the workers' wages, and you said, 'There hasn't been much attrition in your family till now.'

Attrition. Not 'death' because the word 'death' doesn't convey what death actually does, how it wears away at, abrades and erodes the wholeness of the family.

In between these thoughts, I am trying to focus on my work, but I can't worry about it too much, not with Sal's health so precarious.

Now tonight I seem to have cracked a tooth on a seed – I always crunch right through the cores of apples, rejecting only the stalks. I'll have to go to the dentist: time I don't have to spare.

Friday 23rd August
11.55 pm

Today I am just an uncle who thinks his niece is killing herself. There is help available, therapists etc, for eating disorder children. But I've been reluctant to take that step in case it pushes her further. It's as if I'm afraid that by saying aloud, 'You have a problem,' I will make the problem worse.

Which it could hardly be. This morning Sal had a small bowl of Beth's Special K diet cereal. No sugar. She wanted Beth's fat-free milk but it had gone sour and I arm-wrestled her into 2%. For school lunch I packed, and she ate or threw away, a mini (cocktail sized) muffin and a dry roll. Her bottle of apple juice had been consumed. When she got home, she assented to a tiny Star King apple and more juice. Then for supper, a small bowl of pasta without butter or oil, two slices of cucumber and some fairly nutritious (thicker) fruit juice. Nothing but what I've written here. You've got daughters, you remember how much nine-year-olds eat. They pack it away.

After every eating, Sal sucks in her tummy and makes sure she still gets that hit-the-backbone feel. Worse still, she seems to have lost her sense of humour and fun.

And something else, something that shocks me so much I hardly want to say it, even to you. Sal is spending much longer in the loo than usual, and closes the door each time, whereas before she would innocently have a wee in public view. I confess that I lean against the door, straining to hear sounds of gagging or throwing up, but nothing. Perhaps it is just all the extra juice she has been consuming. If she opens the door suddenly while I am doing this, there will be an accident of tragicomic proportions.

I nearly stumbled straight into Angie as I walked back to the parking lot adjacent to the school this morning. She said, 'Sal's looking very peaky these days, is everything all right? She's lost a lot of weight.' She seemed genuinely concerned.

I said, No, everything is not all right. I am close to breakdown. Sal won't eat. I don't understand it, it was so sudden. But the moment I say that I realise I could look back for months and detect tiny signs – Sal giving up fizzy drinks, for instance, Sal going for a run around the park perimeter after eating a chocolate – which at the time seemed positive. Then Beth going and not coming back when she said she would. Lots of little anxieties, brought on by other girls, about being too plump. Does this really happen to girls so young? She's only nine!

Angie's owl-like eyes listened wisely. I was talking to my enemy, yet finding great comfort in it. 'Oh, it happens to girls younger than her. I had a patient who was five years old and refusing to eat. They do get better, especially the younger ones, and if you catch them in time. Your mind's probably thinking of those skeletal adults you sometimes see, but I promise you there are many who recover. You know I was an anorexic?'

I said I'd heard something to that effect. Will you see her, I asked. Can I bring her to see you?

Angie said she thought I should see a specialist in the field. She gave me a name and number. 'You must be taking strain,' she said. 'Do you want me to phone?' I thanked her and said I'd do it myself.

I phoned Ron and explained that I'd decided to make an appointment with a psychologist on Monday because Sal wasn't eating properly. Ron said shouldn't she just go to a nutritionist? I said I didn't think it was about food. He said he was very busy but that I should phone his wife to see if she had any ideas and perhaps it would be a good idea anyway for Lilian to go along on Monday since Sal was probably just missing having a mother figure around. He also said could he cancel Sal's visit on Sunday as he and Lilian had been invited somewhere fancy for lunch. Though it was difficult, I thanked Ron for this garble and said I'd report back.

I phoned the hotel in Mauritius where Beth will be staying, and left a message for her to phone me. Then I went to the dentist. He moulded some kind of dental putty to fill in the crack, and smoothed it lovingly. 'That'll be good for another thirty thousand chews,' he said.

When I came home with a numb mouth, Mrs Cloete was fetching in the laundry for me. You don't have to do that, I said, it's my job.

'I just thought I'd help,' she said. 'I get very bored.'

I gave her a fresh wad of poems I'd just picked up from my post office box and said, Put a tick on any you enjoyed reading. She looked pleased.

Sal didn't want to play with Harriet this afternoon. When I fetched her from school, I didn't know what to say to her. It's so different from our normal easy chattiness.

At home, she went to her room and looked around it as if she were a stranger. I had followed her, hoping she might suggest a snack herself. She slipped her hand inside the waistband that hung loose from her tunic and looked at me with hollow eyes. I said, Sal, you're making yourself ill, please eat something. She shook her head regretfully.

She asked if she could play a game called The Sims on my computer. The game allows you to create a family, buy them a house, find them jobs, buy stuff. Sal has created a character called Ashraf Honey. He lives on his own and today she made him work like the devil, clocking up $$$ so that she could buy him a black leather recliner. He cried, he remonstrated, but she just kept making him work. I wondered if she was disciplining him the way she disciplines herself.

I have made an appointment with the eating disorder psychologist on Monday. I'll fetch Sal early from school.

116

It is bad and it feels bad.

Once we have stopped doing something that is good for us, how do we start again? After that bad review of *The Secret Life of Things*, I didn't publish poetry again for a long time. I no longer wrote poems, not even ones to put away safely in a drawer where they couldn't be hurt.

I wrote nothing until I started writing for you. The story of our love is the story of a love-letter, broken perforce into daily sections, but in essence an uninterrupted stream from one heart to another.

I left the farm after a year because I was getting no sleep. I had to leave. I was so in love with you, yet I had no idea how to proceed. I'd sit up in my cottage, watching the lights at the big house – your house – going out one by one. I'd hear Theo locking the security gate, locking you in. I didn't know how to reach out to you in order to find out if you reciprocated my feelings.

I'd never been in love before, never felt the urge to seduce a woman, though I'd accepted their advances. As a young boy, Beth and her friends had made me join their games of spin-the-bottle. They practised their flirting techniques on me. I learnt that if you did nothing for long enough, a woman's curiosity would overpower her. She'd come up like a lioness and give one a friendly bat on the tail.

When I came back from the army, Monica was the lioness. I would sit quietly in the study editing MA dissertations for well-off students, keeping my mind on footnotes and semicolons and whether it was 'run-off' or 'runoff'. In those days, before everybody had a personal computer, theses were often written in longhand and then copy-typed on electric typewriters. In the course of copy-typing, more errors crept in. Typists sometimes officiously corrected things they didn't like. So one student had written 'Stephen Bantu Biko', and this had been corrected to read 'the Bantu, Stephen Biko'.

Monica would come in and talk to me as I unravelled these tangled messes, perch on the edge of the desk and cross her skirted legs seductively. I was still nervy, plagued by nightmares, so I found her massive self-confidence quite calming. She had some to spare. I never sought her out, or did anything but answer her questions.

One evening I joined a group including Monica and Beth for a drink at the Brass Bell. At closing time I walked Monica to her car politely. She asked if I'd go clubbing with her the next night. I said I didn't think so – I didn't like clubs.

Monica was furious. She scribbled her number on a piece of paper and said I could get hold of her if I ever wanted to see her again. After she roared off, I scrumpled up the paper, thinking that was that. But Monica phoned to apologise, acted as if we'd had a lovers' tiff. I thought, have I missed something here?

I must've missed something, because Monica invited me for supper at her place and after some not very nice food, walked purposefully to the bed in her bachelor flat and took off all her clothes.

How different you were and are. On the day I left the farm, we stood in the tunnel in a sea of roses and I said that despite all the scientific evidence you'd given me to the contrary, I just wanted you to remember that as Gertrude Stein said, a rose is a rose is a rose. You smiled and half touched my shoulder but then withdrew your hand quickly. It was more intimate than if you'd held on firmly. You said, 'I'd like you to write to me – still send me poems. Educate me.' We shook hands.

How did we get here? I sent my first letter in mid-

January last year. In our first letters, the closing salutation is 'Regards' or 'Bye'. How did I lure you into 'Love' and ultimately, 'Your darling'?

There is an art to closeness. I think it begins with a mutual admission of fallibility, telling stories against ourselves –

I'd stupidly put it on 'Rinse', thinking that ...
I hadn't finished it, though I'd promised ...

The intimate correspondent responds by denying our fallibility, affirms our worth –

You are so ...
I love the way you ...

Second is the narrative of childhood –

In our garden there was a well, hidden among Black-eyed Susans, and I would ...
Then the door would close, and I was excluded from ...

Next there is a roundabout discussion of previous disappointment in love and sex –

When I was with Monica I never ...
Though I am present in body, my mind is a rogue ...

And soon afterwards, the opening of secrets –

I wasn't going to tell you this, but ...
I've never told anyone this before ...

I remember your first admission of an 'us'; and your first acknowledgement that receipt of my letters was very important to you. To this was appended an ingenuous apology for writing so frequently –

So I was delighted to find a letter from you waiting here ...

I see that I appear to be writing to you every day. I hope I am not keeping you from ...

You admitted this, I think, because I told you how inexplicably happy I suddenly felt –

These days I wake up smiling ...

(Yes, I was secretly singing all those songs from the 1930s.)

Throughout, as a matter of course, we spoke the dialogue that is normally under erasure –

When he said that, I felt secretly stung, though I pretended nonchalance.

Having to listen to her was like being forced to eat pot-scourer scum.

I was so embarrassed, I wanted to dig a shallow hole and cover myself with grass cuttings, but I put on a brave face.

And I thought, 'I must divorce him while there is still time to have a life.'

So I came to know you properly, over a matter of mere weeks. By the end of February, we were shyly holding hands in syntax and hinting at more. I kept waiting for you to slap me down, saying, 'Now you've gone too far!'

But you didn't. I said I wanted to stroke your hair – you accepted that. I said I wanted to press my lips to the vein in your temple – you accepted that.

You said you knew it was wrong to think of me as often as you did, but that you could not help it. And I sent you Alice Meynell's poem, 'I must not think of thee', which I think she wrote when she was in love with a Catholic priest. You replied, 'That's it, that's exactly it.' (Though I am no priest.)

Boldly, I wrote, quoting Roethke:

I knew a woman, lovely in her bones

You said you loved Roethke, but would I please send you some of my own poems? You would like to see anything I had written.

It is a turning point for any writer, the day he meets a sympathetic audience, someone who urges him to write, who responds to what he has written, someone who actually *wants him to write*. You were more than reader – you were (and remain) mentor and muse. 'There is a poem in that paragraph,' you would write, and only then could I see that yes, of course there was. I would set it out, work on it, send it to you for comment.

I was publishing again. And I was writing well because you were there, I was writing *for you*, as I still do. I only care that my words draw back a curtain *for you*; the wider world who reads them when they are published is only overhearing a private conversation.

You came to me like a continental film after a long enforced diet of Hollywood trash.

Of course by now we wanted a chance to meet in the flesh. You were driving in to town for the Kirstenbosch sale in March, to buy Leucadendron and Leucospermum with flashy names like Tango, Scarlet Ribbon, Inca Gold, Red Gem. Theo accepted that in order to get the best plants you needed to be in the queue early; he was amenable to the idea of you staying overnight in a bed and breakfast in Newlands.

I convinced you that while nothing might happen between us, we should have a double room in case we did want to be alone. It seemed crude to express it any other way. You let me phone the B&B to change your booking. When the receptionist answered, I confess I was thinking so passionately about what I'd like to do to your naked body, lovingly naming its parts in my best Anglo-Saxon, that I half whispered an obscenity into her ear. 'What?' she asked. I said I was just calling my cat.

As you know, I have always loathed clichés. But in the week running up to our first sexual encounter, I thought almost exclusively in clichéd pornographic images. Except they were not, because you were in them. The word I used then to describe my feelings for you was not 'love' but 'adore'. I adored you, worshipped the happy ground you stepped on.

I thought of soaping you down in a shower – I had lots of shower daydreams. I also had the compulsory naked-beside-the-fireplace fantasy. No, but the undressing is so sexy, I had to quickly rewind that one, and start with your imagined underwear, though not too much of it, not with this urgency. A satiny garment with you bare beneath it to my surprised and delighted touch. A thin black strap over your shoulder that I slip off and then I follow with my fingertips the soft swell on either side of your cleavage. We take off the petticoat together. *Oh, my America, my Newfoundland!* I stroke the heavy undersides of your breasts while my tongue moves on your exposed nipples. I kiss you and then kneel before you, running my hands down the all of you. Your knees fall open, vulnerable as a starfish. I watch your eyes close with pleasure. I rim your other mouth. Now my fingers slip into you, curled and secret. Meeting a little resistance at first, I persist, like someone widening a declivity in the wet sand of a beach. Then, when I feel a closing of the rings like a murmured warning, when you are quite desperate, calling my name, I thrust my rampant self into you. Your hips and mine, rising and falling in a cadence more ancient than pentameter.

Oh yes I forgot, and there was a crackling log fire, and gorgeous eastern rug.

Reality is quite different. It is better.

I remember that moment when you walked into the Coffee Bean where we'd arranged to meet before checking into our honeymoon room together. Hoping to look debonair, caught casually in the act of reading, I'd taken along a copy of Antjie Krog's *Down To My Last Skin*. I thought our meeting would be like a melting of the final barrier separating us: touch. But when you came in and recognised me, you looked as though you wanted to run away. I was suddenly scared. I thought, if she leaves now, my life hereafter will be darkness.

You sat down opposite me, ordered tea. Everything was magnified. I saw goosebumps on your forearms. I reached out to put my hands over yours. It was as though you merely suffered this intimacy. Off the page, we were so awkward. Worse still, terror had chased out desire. I became self-conscious, feeling the extra tyre of flesh around my middle where a six-pack should be. I knew I must look a pathetic, unromantic figure: nothing like Theo's iron-hard body. For your part, I could see that the enormity of what you'd done had sunk in: *I've agreed to sleep with this man, this younger man who now seems a complete stranger*. Yet we were not strangers, had

123

exchanged the secrets that bind people together. There was one thing in our favour at that moment: we still trusted one another. Perhaps that's what prevented you from bolting.

I stood briefly at the window of your Isuzu discussing directions before we drove to the B&B in tandem. I thought how softly rounded your arms looked on the steering wheel, but even that frightened me. Physically, you were so ... feminine. In a good way: curvy, enigmatic – but in a way I'd never encountered sexually before. I knew you professionally, intellectually, emotionally, but – what was it? It was your dress and delicate shoes, I realised. I had never seen you look so vulnerable; I was used to your farm gear – jeans and wellington boots. Two thoughts came to me, crashing against each other. I am in love with her. She will never leave Theo.

When we arrived at the guesthouse, we were shown straight in (it seemed) to the double bed. I carried our bags while you walked ahead with the proprietor. I saw you glance at the bed and your hand went up to your throat. I thought, she is going to faint. Luckily, there were those French doors, so you were able to avoid the bed and go straight out into the fresh air. A door closed discreetly. We were alone. You looked up at the mountain view, thinking, as you told me later, Oh God, oh God. I came out and leant a little bit against the wooden railing next to you, with my hands in the front pockets of my jeans to steady me. Everything depended on what I said next. So I ventured: Are you feeling overwhelmed? Do you feel we've been a bit precipitate? Do I seem strange to you? Does it suddenly seem too real to you, now that it's happening? I tried to put into words how you felt.

You nodded, looking down at the ground. You told me that you'd never slept with another man, apart from

Theo. The early lovers, the ones you'd mentioned to me in your letters, were strictly kissing boyfriends. This was by way of explaining that you thought perhaps other, more experienced women might take this romantic assignation of ours in their stride, but that you found you couldn't. Though as long as we were only writing about it, you'd felt that you could do this thing too, this impetuous taking of a lover. You said you'd felt so excited, so exhilarated as you drove over Sir Lowry's Pass to meet me earlier that day. But now you couldn't explain how you felt. 'Oh, I'm rambling, I'm incoherent. I'm sorry,' you said.

I listened. Then I said, Well we are here now, and we're together, and I'm happy about that. It's all I need. We can just sleep chastely next to each other, if you like. And you nodded again, shyly. Relieved, you rambled some more. I said, I hope your qualms won't stop us from having a good dinner together and enjoying one another's company. You said, 'Of course not,' and smiled. You know I like a good meal. But I was also trying to be wise. I was searching my mind for unused resources.

I drove us to a Japanese restaurant – Wasabi – in your Isuzu. You'd said, 'Could we go somewhere exotic? Theo's idea of going out to eat is meat and three veg.' While you were in the bathroom, I made an emergency call to Ryno, who tipped me off about the place. I remember laughing as Ryno asked me, 'What are the specs here, John, give me the specs.' And I had to say, first date, request for exotic, very beautiful, poet besotted.

It was your first taste of sashimi (my second – not that I said so); you couldn't work out the chopsticks at first; you dipped your raw tuna in too much wasabi and nearly choked. We drank Pongracz and laughed. Gradually, stiffness fell away and we became more and more ourselves. The personae that we knew through words started to fill out these slightly alien bodies, until the two came together and up to date, words and self: John and Theresa.

I liked the way you enthused over the food, the decor, the 'real Japanese' rolling sushi behind the counter. You made me feel like a man who knows what he's doing, knows how to treat a woman right – urbane, suave, *savoir vivre*. None of which I am, I know, but who doesn't live for those fleeting moments when we convince others of our fantasy lives?

I liked the way you ate tiny morsels at first, as if you were nervous of the salmon. Then it grew on you, you relaxed, said you'd only ever eat your fish raw from now on. I liked the way the champagne made you slightly flirtatious. You weren't looking down and nodding now, but straight into my eyes, laughing. In conversation we retraced the steps of our love: that was good.

When we got back into your 4x4 after the crowded restaurant, there was another moment of shyness between us. We were alone. The cab was a small, dark, private interior where something like a kiss might take place. It came on me like pain how much I wanted to make love to you. But what could I do about that? Even though I suspected you might have changed your mind, or at least opened it to the possibility, I'd given you my word, promised that we could sleep chastely next to one another. I thought, if she puts her hand on my knee, or kisses my cheek, then I'll know she is making an advance.

Again we entered our double room. You sat on the edge of the bed, tightly wrapped in a beautiful shawl. You seemed at a loss, not in a hurry about toothbrushes, not covering up the moment with bustle. I sat down next to you and very gently took your hand in mine. Then very softly, not wanting to disturb you, I said, And what happens now? Perhaps it was the responding pressure of your hand, perhaps you tilted your face up towards mine, or perhaps we read one another's minds, but I kissed you then. Have I ever told you what a sweet, tentative kisser you are?

Getting inside the shawl was like trying to do (undo?) origami. There is more, but I must stop here.

We spent the night together. Because it was hot, and because however much in love one is, sleeping with an unaccustomed presence is difficult, I got up in the early hours to open the French doors and to look at the quiet sky. You joined me, standing naked, leaning back against my naked torso, our arms entwined, and I said I never want to be parted from you. You said it would be difficult, but you did really want to leave Theo, you meant to do it. You said that. I often wonder about the things people say on their first night of love. I still mean what I said that night; I don't know what happened to your conviction.

After that we met when we could, though not for a whole night again until last year's botanical sale. It is the only time in my life that I have felt excited by shrubs. In between, we still wrote. Daily, and always alert for opportunities, however brief, to meet. Perforce, we mastered the art of the quickie. Your letters to me – even just the sight of your name on my computer or cellphone screen, would arouse me. When we couldn't meet, we'd describe what we'd like to do to one another. You said the Irish had a slang term for a sexy man – 'a ride' – and that I was 'a ride'. I think I had the world's first two-week erection. I'd go out for a pub lunch with Ryno and he'd tell me, 'Get that fucking grin off your face.'

By April I was writing incendiary stuff on the topic –

Convergence
When I am millimetres from your skin
after miles of tedious geography in between;
When parting is mere minutes away
but merging only seconds;
When I am, at last, first on your list;
When I am hard, ready to take and slake
but also to be made hungry again;
When life pauses, fleetingly,
at the door of our private room;
(When coming means going
but there's no stopping coming);
Then I am
the unearthed electricity
of breaking weather.

Not surprising that a few months after I wrote and sent 'Convergence', Theo rumbled us. It didn't take much sleuthing. Apparently, you printed out my poems, placed them in a folder on your desk. Already suspicious about your earnest checking for new emails, Theo was drawn to your office and your desk as one is to a secret. It's so easy to flip open a cardboard file – it hardly seems like spying.

A husband reading a poem like 'Convergence', knowing or even just suspecting it was from his wife's lover, would feel quite sick. Angry and sick. Theo spat vitriol at me, so you say. Then he summoned your daughters from their homes in the north to give you a talking to: the moralistic young allowed to reprove their elders. A female version of that painful scene from *Hamlet* –

... speak no more,
Thou turn'st my eyes into my very soul,

128

And there I see such black and grained spots
As will not leave their tinct.

That's when you met me with your knitting quills, and we lapsed into this uneasy pact, of rare, chaste meetings. And the letters. You would not give these up. You acknowledge Theo's rights over your body, but not over your heart or mind. Theo believes that all contact between us has ceased. He is deceived. Still, this is for you a bearable deception.

I can't help feeling that what you are doing is simply failing to make a decision, frittering away your life like a dilettante and his inheritance. The moment I say that, write that, I know it applies even more to me than it does to you.

Today's irony. Mrs Cloete came in during the plain pasta supper with a poem she liked. The title is very good:

Why my life is like Retreat station
'All change, all change,'
and we board another train
or wait, ruminating on insults
surely meant for someone else.
The timetable is the roughest guide
to what you might expect. Peering
down the track's as good a guess as any
as to what will happen next. Time's a
permanent junction. The Cape Flats line
divides a life of howling wind from one
of shelter, but those of us who always seek
the same safe destination are bound to face
defeat. Go on then, race to meet
those whom you must meet,
but recall Retreat.

Who is it by, I asked. Mrs Cloete fumbled for the covering letter. 'Tizzy Clack,' she said.

That bitch, I said. I told Mrs Cloete about the 'himself, himself, himself' review of *The Secret Life of Things*, the one that sent me spiralling down into not writing again.

'So are you going to reject her poem because of that?' asked Mrs Cloete.

No, I said, but uncertainly. Mrs Cloete looked at me inquisitorially, forcing me to wonder: Have I got to thirty-seven and not learnt how to crush my own vindictiveness? I read the poem again. I'll publish it, I said at last.

Mrs Cloete asked did I have any more poems for her to vet. 'It's better than playing patience,' she said. I said I'd be sure to pass her compliment on to the poets.

My breathing feels tight; it feels as though someone has kicked me in the chest. Last night long strands of phlegm snagged my throat, causing spasms of coughing. I couldn't sleep even though I was so tired. I tried propping myself up with cushions, but my lungs continued to agitate about the trickle from above. At last I got up, found a cough sweet and lay there sucking it till my chest calmed and I dropped off. There was still a brittle disc of sweet left on my tongue when I woke.

And I am permanently hungry. I am trying to eat as little as Sal, certainly in her presence. It seems wrong to be robust in the face of someone who has chosen wasting. But I need more food than this.

The menus are making me hungry. I haven't told you. A new restaurant is opening at the harbour and the proprietor, a guy called Ferdinand, thinks it will be really great to have rhyming menus composed by a local poet, for recitation by the waiters. I have to get them ready by next week. And he's paying! We may yet be able to fix the cracks. Here's the gravadlax starter:

I'm rhyming salmon, Norwegian,
With salmon, Cape region
We cure it with rock salt
(That's not the rock's fault.)

The chef is not rusty
He serves it with rosti
You'll love it, you'll fetish
He lays it in crème fraiche.
You're right if you're guessing
There's a sweet mustard dressing.

It's a new form of prostitution.

Saturday 24th August
10.58 pm

I have had brief respite (moments) from Sal. Her friend
Harriet came to play today and ate twelve cocktail
viennas on a kebab skewer, dipped in tomato sauce. Sal
was moved to eat seven. Now I have started to count
food.

Beth phoned early in a state of utter fury – not at
me, but at her mogul boyfriend who doesn't want to cut
their holiday short in Mauritius so that she can return
to look after Sal. 'Don't let the kid manipulate you,' he
apparently said.

'Kid' and 'manipulate' are like dirty words around
here. What my mother would have called 'common'. Beth

says she's moved into another hotel room at her own expense and is trying to get her flight changed.

Earlier I broached the subject of Monday's appointment with Sal, using the word-mincing script dictated to me by the psychologist on the phone. Namely that because she'd seemed unhappy lately, she was going to talk to a lady on Monday afternoon.

'Oh, a psychologist? About my eating problem?' pipes up Sal and proceeds to tell Harriet and Hannelie with pride. 'Can I get emotional?' she asks, cheerfully.

She seemed so positive about the prospect of therapy that I decided to make slow-cooked lamb knuckles in red wine and tomatoes. Well, I like slow-cooked lamb. Hannelie helped me brown the onions and the meat in batches. Then I put the whole lot in a clay baker with its lid on and put it in the oven at 140 degrees.

Hannelie and I were drinking tea when quite unexpectedly, the poet Vusi – the one whose turgid poems I rejected – pitched up. His arrival was signalled by a frenzy of barking from Ryno's dog. When Sir Nicholas had calmed down enough for us to speak, Vusi greeted me politely, called me brother, said 'I'm Vusi Gunguluza.'

I said yes, I know, I met you at Café Moroka last year. He said he didn't think I'd remember.

I was nervous that this was an umbrage call. Maybe it was. It was hard to work out his tone. He stood there in his dreadlocks and groovy clothes, chuckling. At what, I don't know.

Well, come in, I said, this is Hannelie. Would you like some tea?

Hannelie said she'd go make a fresh pot and check on the children.

After more pleasantries, Vusi said he'd really like to talk

to me about poetry. He thought maybe there were some problems with meaning and reception that had caused his poems to be rejected.

Meaning and reception? I didn't want to beat around this bush.

So, would you like to talk about the poems you sent, the ones I rejected, I asked.

'Yes,' he said. 'I must say I was very surprised, very surprised about the ones you rejected.'

I rejected all of them, I reminded him.

'You rejected all of them,' he said, 'and that made me deeply sad. I wasn't expecting that.'

I asked him if he'd given some thought to the more positive aspect of my letter, where I'd enquired after his extemporaneous verse.

'Yes, yes, thank you for that, that was very positive,' said Vusi. 'But now my extemporaneous verse is very, you know, extemporised.'

I said I realised there were problems with recording impromptu performances, but that I was confident they could be overcome. I just have to say that I think that's where your gift lies, I said.

'Ah, my gift,' he nodded.

Hannelie came in with the tea. 'The children are playing such a funny game,' she said, 'you must come and listen.'

It turned out that Harriet and Sal were recording a spoof radio programme. Harriet introduced Sal as an expert on snakes. Sal said that the snake she was handling was very unique – and you could see her mentally searching for a unique quality to ascribe to a snake – because 'this snake knows about politics!' We all laughed.

Vusi asked if he could be a guest on their programme.

Harriet pressed Record and announced, 'And today in the studio we're very lucky to have the poet Vusi Gorgonzola. Vusi – hi!'

Vusi thanked the radio host for inviting him on board, and asked her how she was. Harriet said she was in excellent health and that she could see Vusi was 'relaxed and blooming'. The listeners were longing to hear him do his thing, she gushed.

The moment he held the mike, I could see him fall into character. He began slowly, seemed to find thought inside the rhyme. I suspected he was using the refrain as a brief island to regroup his thoughts before pressing on with complete assurance. This is what I have transcribed:

Give the poet what he needs
certain sad repeated beats
on which he feeds
give the poet what he needs
some slow anthem's lead
the spirit freed.

Give the poet what he needs
a certain scene once seen
nineteen eighty-three
clean pairs of heels
in a dusty shebeen
leaping sleep
in a lean-to
asleep on concrete
without a key.
Ah, give the poet what he needs
harvest of reeds
whispered creeds
windswept seeds

certain prophecies in beads
certain thorny trees
home-talking Lusisiki

barefoot impis of history.

Give the poet what he needs
certain roads that lead
certain vagrant's pleas
give the poet what he needs
give the poet what he needs

I want to use your poem, I said afterwards. I want to copy it down from the tape and publish it.

'Okay,' said Vusi. 'Okay.' The diphthong was drawn out.

You sound reluctant, I said.

'Ja, I'm just worried that you have an agenda for me. I mean, there are certain things you want from me, maybe as a black poet, you know, "reeds" and so forth, and then that poem fulfils those criteria.'

But what about those poems you sent me, I asked, with all the 'thees' and 'thous'? Aren't you also adopting a persona there?

I was trying to argue delicately, because I was trying to catch a poem, trying to avoid the race card at all costs. I just wanted Vusi to let me publish 'Give the Poet What He Needs'. I didn't want to have to discuss the purpose of poetry or anyone's agenda.

'Well, yes, a persona that is part of my tradition,' said Vusi. 'It is African tradition to use poetry – you know – formally. The main purpose of poetry is not to entertain, but to educate.'

The blazes with education, I said. If it comes to

expectations, then what you've just said shows you're very happy to work within other people's expectations. When you were speaking into the mike just now, you were doing your thing. That's what poets do. Let me publish it. C'mon.

Vusi looked at me and laughed. 'Okay,' he said. 'Oh and by the way, on another topic, have you got a job for my sister?'

I was completely dumbstruck. Vusi fixed me with his big brown eyes, watched me stutter and splutter about how we couldn't afford a domestic worker right now.

'What kind of work does your sister do?' asked Hannelie.

Vusi started to roar with laughter – quite different from the insinuating chuckle of our opening conversation. He was relishing my discomfort.

'Good question, good question, Hannelie. In fact, my sister is a hydro-geologist,' he said. 'She's not looking for domestic work. I'm just joking with you, my friend!'

I laughed a hollow laugh, even slapped my thigh to show how funny I thought this joke was. But I didn't think it was funny. Bringing in his sister's occupation was irrelevant. This is about power, I thought, and I've just lost it.

Hannelie gathered up her belongings and went to fetch Harriet from Sal's room. Vusi said he should be going too. No, stay, I said, insincerely, can't I offer you a beer?

Vusi settled down comfortably with an Amstel. I decided we were going to drink towards intimacy, achieve male bonding through alcohol. Then we'd sit down to my hearty stew and Vusi would discover that he liked me. He would say something like 'You're a good man, John,' when we finally parted.

But after one beer, Vusi said he'd be going now, he

had friends to meet in Lansdowne. A poet's group, in fact. Again I had that odd sensation of being left out, even though I don't particularly like the idea of writers' groups. If I wanted to join, I suppose they'd have to have me. Vusi didn't say anything about me being a good man. Just, 'Cheers, John,' and he was gone.

I hoped Sal would join me and tuck into the lamb. No, she wasn't hungry. She assented to a few grains of rice and then slipped off to watch TV. I sat in lonely state at the table, getting delicious fatty gravy all over my unshaven chin, sucking the marrow, quaffing an entire bottle of Nederburg Baronne.

I thought how I would not like you to see me now. It's not impossible. I mean, you have in the past popped in unexpectedly. Twice you've come in here with only five minutes to spare me. Once at eight in the morning when I was wearing an old grubby towelling robe of Beth's and trying to clean the washing machine filter. Theo was having some kind of medical check-up at Constantiaberg Medi-Clinic, so you just had enough time to say hello. Hello! On another occasion you were showing some overseas visitors around and you'd left them in a curio shop to scoot up here. Is that really enough for you, I wonder, to see me in passing? A glimpse, a peck on the cheek, my hands still full of wet grey washing machine wool? I'm a poet, for God's sake. I need the full moon rising in a pink sky behind the money tree. I ache for you.

I was feeling quite morose when a poem by John Lennon came into my head. I can't remember where he put the line breaks, but it went something like, 'I sat belonely down a tree, humbled, fat and small'. If John Lennon felt that, belonely and fat, then I am all right.

Later I wrote an email to Tizzy Clack, accepting (graciously, nay gallantly) her poem about Retreat station. I said I thought the poem was marvellous and that 'we' loved it. The 'we' refers to Mrs Cloete and me, but I'd like Ms Clack to feel awed by the presence of a committee. I felt noble, clean and free from resentment, even though secretly I hoped she felt terrible for her bad review three years ago.

Laugh, Theresa.

There was an email from Vera, attaching the opening paragraphs of her novel. Did I think they were any good? I was to be completely honest:

The sign said 'Keep off: Dune Rehabilitation in Progress', but the thin fencing had been desecrated by the tides and she went with Nature rather than the municipality. Standing on the rise with the thin grasses tickling her ankles – castaway – it struck her that she had read a book about this very thing. A woman on a beach with her family, goes for a walk on her own and then just carries on walking. Buys a ticket and starts a new life in a new town. And, wait, yes, she'd seen a film, even more like this than the book. About an Italian woman whose tour bus moves on, leaving her behind, and she takes the gap, begins a new, much sweeter life in Venice. Afterwards, when the credits came up, Delia had wanted to stay on in the cinema, to keep on living inside the film and not have to go home.

She sat down to get out of the wind, her back against the dune, basking in the last of the sun, letting its warmth defy the onset of evening. It occurred to her that the synchronicity between her life and art was less surprising than it might at first seem. After all, weren't women always being left, forgotten, taken for granted?

Women, with their romances and their longings, were
always living parallel lives, slipping between the scenes
of real sex, where your husband reaches a hand out from
behind his newspaper to tweak your nipple, and fantasy
sex, where a lover without a face takes an infinitely long
time and great pleasure in tracing every contour of your
body. She lay there, thinking that thought for a while.
Her eyes were closed and she could hear the regular
crash-retreat of the wave, the sucking as it pulled out,
then the moment of silence, then the sand-smacking
impact as it broke. Water was very sexy too. Today when
they were swimming, she had wanted Ken to find her
in the water, put his arms around her, gently bob her
up and down. But he swam straight past her, directly
to the yellow buoy and back again. A quick shower and
he stood shaking his wet hair on the beach, mission
accomplished. She had no allure, Delia decided, she
gave off no siren call.

After a bottle of wine, I was tempted to say that my
honest opinion was that it wasn't fair to make me do this.
I don't want to read other people's writing, I thought. I
just want to write.

But then I thought, maybe I could get Vera to subscribe
to *The Unofficial View*. Also, maybe I should just try to
be a helpful person. I wrote:

Dear Vera

I like the dunes and Ken and the interior monologue
and the way you're clearly writing about something
close to your heart and a setting you know well. But the
'women ... women' generalisations worry me – I'd like to
feel we've moved beyond these Venus/Mars polarities. I

also think that the art/life synchronicity is a bit strained.
Rather don't point it out? If there really is already a good
book and a good film on the topic, aren't you inviting
unflattering comparisons? Try to make the opening
sentence contain some essential truth that the rest of
your novel will play with or expand on or unravel. The
Nature/Municipality joke is half-hearted. You don't want
Delia to alienate readers (eg those who worry about dune
rehabilitation) so early on. Generally, you're quite hard
on her. The nipple tweak is eina.

Try it as a 22-line poem?

Regards
John

Meanwhile I'm still working on the menu. The first main
course option is *half a free range partially deboned
Peking duck roasted till crispy, with a Van Der Hum and
Orange sauce. Served on a bed of pesto potato mousse.*
This is what I've produced:

You're in luck, we've half a duck
Before you own it we'll part debone it.
It sings of Peking,
and hums Van der Hum.
It's crispy, it's risky
But come on, get frisky.

It lies on a bed that's designed to seduce:
Of potato and pesto a soft creamy mousse.

(I can't believe I'm doing this.)

I think I'm getting gout. Last night my big toe felt irritated and kept attacking the long thin one that lives next to it. I hate the thought of giving up red wine. Perhaps it is not gout, yet. Also, my ear is on fire with itchiness. If I could look in there, as I'd like to do, I'd see inflamed skin and flaking patches of eczema. I've coated it with Bactroban, but it may need cortisone.

This morning Sal ate her bird rations again: half a piece of toast; naartjie segments.

We took Sir Nicholas for a walk on the section of Fish Hoek beach where dogs are allowed. Although it is usual to find bits of driftwood, especially in winter, today something quite unexpected had washed up: a huge, solid squared off trunk of rare African hardwood, its illegal journey to Europe or America interrupted by high seas. I thought how this mysterious heft must have wrenched away one stormy night from its straining pirate bonds, rolled overboard and coasted here, to this amazed resting place. *Stolen from Africa.* That's a good line. Bob Marley. This tree does not know what it will mean to me, how it will stay with me. Or perhaps it does.

Probably the most intense religious moment of my life was hearing the voice of a piece of wood speak to me as a child. It was a solemn Good Friday mass and an actor had agreed to read 'The Dream of the Rood'. He stood in the organ-loft, concealed, so that one could only hear this deep, resonant, disembodied voice. I truly believed it was the wood of the cross speaking: *I did not dare to topple over. They pierced me with dark nails; the wounds are visible upon me, gaping malicious gashes. I did not dare*

141

to harm any of them. They humiliated us both together.

Theatre, pure theatre – what all religion should be. An awakening to the mystery of life. An admission that though we crawl along on the ground, our souls remember flight.

Immanence
Mostly it's mere maintenance –
sweeping, scraping, patching,
shovelling, packing, heaving,
fetching, lifting, carrying,
buying, feeding, replacing,
wiping, scrubbing, cleaning,
sanding, buffing, shining,
hanging, drying, folding,
soaping, rinsing, smoothing.

But still the longing for
birth, change, growth,
holy, greater, further,
sky, flight, apex,
oneness, idyll, bliss,
incorporeal, sublime,
epiphany, immanence.

Striding out across hardened stretches of sand at low tide this morning, we overheard snippets of other lives. 'Then the mongoose ... back from East London ... a kind of sponge and ... to the doctor ... so what could she do?' Like a child's game of funny faces, building up a grotesque mask from cuttings.

Sir Nicholas entertained himself by sniffing the behinds of other dogs quite obscenely, or by raising angry lips to expose dripping canines to rivals, or by engaging in quick bursts of play with little fluff balls. I noticed how we beach walkers feign disinterest in one another. With each overtaking, there is a moment's hesitation, a fumbling towards greeting, a half smile, a mumble.

On Fish Hoek beach it comes to me that there are couples who have stayed married, couples still holding hands: they make it seem possible. Also, there are people here who have made a decent old age, have kept trim and vigorous. At the corner, the perennial bathers wade out in AP Jones swimwear, stoical, heroic, with dim echoes of the evacuation from Dunkirk.

I was in this state of deep peace when I saw an elderly woman and her terrier approaching from the opposite direction. The terrier's back went up as it bared fangs at Sir Nicholas. Our dog raced ahead in a mock attack. The terrier lacked irony, and launched himself into battle. The two of them kept going at one another, snarling and nipping. I charged over and used the leash as a whip to subdue Sir Nicholas and then quickly clip him back into restraint. I probably hit the other dog accidentally while I was about it. The indignant owner certainly thought so. She stood there cuddling her nasty-faced mutt and giving me a thousand words on my dog's 'bullying' and 'savage' behaviour. 'I saw his jaws sink into Jim's flesh!' she cried.

I apologised, even though I thought her dog was as much at fault. What I really wanted to do was scream: Shut up, bitch! I've been left with this fucking dog to look after, my niece is starving to death, I can't find enough good poems, the woman I love won't have me, my house leaks, I'm only just managing to put one foot in front of the other and keep going, now you come along with your insane accusations!

She was still lecturing me. 'Your type of dog needs to be kept on a leash at all times. You're just spoiling it for the rest of us!'

I wanted to tell her that she had just ruined the reputation of Fish Hoek, that all my fond thoughts of lasting marriages, AP Jones, Dunkirk, and sporting octogenarians had been dispelled by her intolerance. But I said nothing. I need to get angry, need to stand up for myself. Instead, I'm becoming more and more passive.

When we got home, Sal said she had a tummy-ache. I said people who don't eat do get sore tummies. Would she eat anything? We bargained for a while before she settled on an apple cut into quarters and a tiny Chinese bowl of raisins. Then I made up a bed for her in front of the TV and brought her a hot water bottle. I wanted to go upstairs and work, but she seemed to want me there. So I sat next to her with my notebook and pencil and made a list of the poems I have so far:

Red Moffat – 'Haiku #1' and 'Haiku #2'
Girisha Naidoo – 'Light Falls' and 'Refraction'
Primrose Mkhaliphi – 'The Samaritans at Home'
Vusi Gunguluza – 'Give the Poet What He Needs'
Tizzy Clack – 'Why My Life is Like Retreat Station'
Damon Pasquale (Mountain Club) – 'Tortoise'
Trevor Murray (Mountain Club) – 'Rain Walk: Table Mountain'

That's only nine. Hell. I need at least another sixteen. Better chivvy Mrs Cloete to find some, I thought.

I was pleased to find her hard at work, poring over poems with her big bifocals. Not a bad system we've got, I was moved to say. 'Got a mad sister?' she asked. Not a bad system, I repeated, loudly. Her own mishearing seemed to amuse her. 'Could we put in one called "Poetry of the Deaf"?' she asked.

Sal is here now, playing on the floor with her dolls. She came in just now with a bag of Barbie accessories, saying she doesn't want to be alone.

I think about how good and gentle you are, and long especially for that gentleness. I visualise you. My usual picture of us is lying quietly with you in my arms, no clothes, and my upper arm (my right arm) partly covers your breast. Or actually partly doesn't.

I re-read your last letters and speculate intensely over a word or a phrase you've used and try to guess your state of mind, heart, soul there or between the lines. You say that ordinary, innocuous words have become taboo between you and Theo. You can't say 'email' or 'poem' or refer to any suburb of Cape Town further south than Wynberg.

At least I can say your name aloud, occasionally. Beth knows about you, and Ryno too. I love it when Beth asks, 'How is Theresa?' Then I can boast of your successes, how you're getting more overseas and local orders because your roses are so perfect; how you help me see the poems inside my thoughts; the kind things you do for your workers. I like to tell Beth and Ryno about Frikkie, who keeps expecting you to upgrade or replace or modify his wheelchair. He really is quite imperious with you. But you humour him.

An email from Vera:

Dear John

Thanks for the advice. Have reduced two turgid paragraphs to the following Haiku:

145

Left behind by Ken
Barbie opens plastic arms
for other sea-men

Regards
Vera

I replied:

Dear Vera

Can I publish it?

John

The menu work continues. Now I'm onto the catch of the day: *An oven baked fillet of fresh line fish topped with a herb and lemon sambal on a bed of fragrant Basmati rice.*

This is the rhyme. May it pay for a section of the new gutter we need:

Our line fish, fresh filleted
Has asked to be billeted
With you.

It came here quite naked
But we'll soon oven-bake it
And send it to gambol
With a herb lemon sambal
Then let it win like karate
On a bed of basmati.

(What if real poems desert me, and I become a poetaster?)

Another bad night. I had a terrible dream that a cat had climbed through the window and had stuck its claws into my back while I slept, though of course I was still asleep as I thought this. As I struggled to pull it off, it lacerated my hands. By the time I had wrenched it painfully free of one hand, it would be hooked to the other. I had it hanging over the windowsill, was trying to force it to let go and drop down, which I could only do by bringing the sash window down on its back and squashing it. Thus I was wide awake, crazed, when Sal came to my bed at about two in the morning. We tried sleeping top-to-toe for a while, but I needed to toss and turn, so I eventually crept out to *her* bed. I believe parents do this kind of thing.

I left Sal with the psychologist, Claire Blake, today. All the way to Tokai my right eye and eyebrow twitched and flickered with nerves. But when we pulled in at her untarred driveway, the scene was so charming and bucolic that my spirits lifted and my eye settled down.

I hope you have read at least one of the Madeline books by Ludwig Bemelmans. The eating disorder psychologist Angie recommended is what I imagine Miss Clavell would be like if she lived here, now, in Cape Town at the turn of the century. Miss Clavell, you remember, is the thin, wedge-shaped French governess who rushes at an angle across the page in quick brushstrokes, always in some consternation over what has befallen the twelve little girls in two straight lines.

Well, just like Miss Clavell, Claire Blake lives in a tall, thin double-storey house covered in vines and I don't doubt the Spanish ambassador lives next door, because next door is one of those squat, sprawling white upper Tokai mansions that only foreigners with euros can afford.

At first I was endeared to Claire's eccentricity. She shares her thin, quirky forest home with two horses, two dogs and three children. One of each species is a bit sickly. There is a horse who was in a car accident once and who kicks and starts a lot, and one of the dogs has hip dysplasia and one child has a nose that never stops dripping and a very adenoidal manner of speech.

Though she reminds me of Miss Clavell, there are no straight lines in Claire's house. Her husband is an architect, but apparently he doesn't use a spirit level. Perhaps Claire is his spirit level – she is quite thin and flat.

Sal immediately relaxed and started to play with the dogs. I thought Claire might ask me to stay but she just said I was to come back in an hour. She pointed out a side door with a large old school bell attached nearby. 'Come and ring loudly on that,' she said, 'and we'll decide whether to let you in.'

To pass the time, I drove to the Constantia mall to have coffee and a large lemon meringue pie at Seattle. When I came back and rang the bell, I could feel that something quite significant had taken place, if only in words. Claire sent Sal off to the paddock with her boys and called me inside.

'It's very unusual for me to be speaking to an uncle,' she said. 'Could neither of Sal's parents be here today? However,' she carried on, hardly giving me a chance, 'Sal is crying for help, there's no doubt about that.'

She proceeded with her analysis. I've probably got the different points mixed up, but this is what I heard.

Apparently Sal shows the classic signs of an addictive personality, something about clinging to the mother and the caregiver (me) and not achieving separation.

I remembered that Sal had watched the video *Dumbo* at least eighty-six times when she was not much more than a toddler. I personally pressed Play on several occasions. Did that count as addiction?

On the one hand, Claire was totally disapproving about me falling asleep next to Sal, on the other she told me I needed to be more demonstrative. Like her, I suppose. 'Give more hugs,' she said.

I said I thought everyone was very free with their hugs these days, and that I didn't think they were sincere. I gathered from her pursed-lipped response that I was down another ten points or so.

'Little Sal needs a lot of love,' she said.

She has no idea, I thought, how much we love Sal or how our complex little family works. She's judging us against a textbook study, in which hugs = love. I began to think that her interesting house and friendly arrangement of children and pets were a sham, that really this woman was deeply conventional. But even as I thought that, I remembered Sal's shrunken-back tummy as she'd pulled on her T-shirt after school. I desperately needed this woman. Claire could say what she liked, be as disapproving as she liked, as long as Sal started eating again.

Now she was asking if I knew how long Beth had breastfed Sal and I said I thought ten months or a year. I couldn't work out from the expression on Claire's face whether ten months was not long enough or perhaps too long, but again I sensed it was the wrong answer. I do remember Beth complaining that Sal would only drink from one breast, causing an uncomfortable lopsidedness, but I decided I wouldn't mention this. Let's not, as they say, go there.

Claire said Sal was the most extraordinary child she'd met. 'Usually, with a child of this age, you'd approach their problems indirectly, through dolls, puppets or a story. But when I asked Sal why she thought she'd been brought to see me, she gave me a perfect summary.'

I waited to hear it, but Claire simply paused and then asked, 'So what is it that you and your sister actually do in these offices of yours?'

I said I was a poetry editor and my sister a draughts-man.

At first Claire seemed sympathetic. How did we manage the housework and our careers as well as caring for Sal?

I said in a jocular way that a lot of the time we didn't manage – that we were lucky that Sal often played on her own or just got on quietly with her homework. That we were silting down under All-Bran boxes but luckily the septuagenarian boarder helped bring the laundry in. I said sometimes when Sal was reading or making something in her room, and Beth and I were working in our offices, it was like Sal was one of us. I said Sal had a very sophisticated grasp of language and joined in adult conversations easily.

Claire raised her eyebrows. Now I'd really stepped into it. 'So, you and Sal's mom expect this nine-year-old child to meet you on an intellectual level?'

But Sal just *does* meet us on an intellectual level, I thought.

'She's a child,' said Claire, 'who's learnt that in order to get your attention and affection she needs to use long words. I notice that while she is physically tiny, she has the vocabulary of a much older child, an adult even. She's competing with your books and your computer screens. But deep down this child is asking you to let her be a child. You have to give her more of your time.'

Riled, I said that Beth and I had to work, we were both freelancers whose income was always precarious. We both work to deadline, often straight through weekends, if we get a chance.

Claire said that while she was studying for her Master's, she only worked when her children were asleep, from 9pm till 3am. Then she'd sleep for three hours, get up and see them off to school, have another nap, and do the housework before they returned. That's brilliant, I said, but I don't think either Beth or I are made of that kind of metal. Or Teflon, I thought.

'Well, then,' said Claire, 'I have two alternatives for you. Either you and your sister rearrange your work commitments dramatically, or I will have to counsel Sal that this is the way things are and she must just accept it.'

She didn't stop there, but went on and on. About how Sal may have chosen food because it's a passive option (not like biting) or because she knew that food played an important role in my life. About how we needed to shake ourselves up and change our arrangements at home. She gave copious examples from her own life and family, her successful juggling of motherhood and career, all of which suggested that if one didn't do it this way one really wasn't doing it right at all.

She asked about my relationship with my mother, with Monica, with Beth. I said it had been really quite peaceful living with these three women; they let me get on with my writing.

I thought this showed how easy-going I was, but Claire came out with: 'So you have a tendency to live like a child in the household, as long as you perceive that someone

151

else is taking responsibility?'

I thought: Who exactly is being analysed here?

She asked me about *The Unofficial View* and about Beth's big project. I explained how absorbing the editing work had been for me, how delighted Beth was to be sought after by high-profile clients.

Claire leant back and said, 'Aahh, so you each have a new baby in your lives, and little Sal is being crowded out. Poor smidgen.'

Smidgen is my word for Sal. Claire knew it. 'That's your word for her, isn't it? I suppose she might think you only like her small.' Oh hell, I thought, what will happen when we aren't allowed to call them our pets, our poppets, our babies, our lambkins?

I was completely unprepared for the way she singled me out; I kept waiting for her to finger some other cause: school, friends, Ron, modern life. I did recognise, however, what her technique was. *Shoot everything that moves and everything until it moves.*

She wanted to get a rise out of me, because it's when we get angry that we most expose ourselves. Maybe, to give her her due, she could see that I was an introvert. She was prodding me to speak. I'm afraid my soul just clammed up. I think Claire wanted me to crack, to break down, because really, she was very pointed, almost redoubling her efforts when I simply mildly agreed that I saw it now: we were the problem. Beth and I needed to give Sal more time.

'Find something to do together that hasn't got anything to do with words, something tactile,' was Claire's parting shot. 'And I'd like to see her again in a week's time. She's got my number so she can phone me any time she likes.'

I wondered whether she thought Sal was an abused child who needed a help-line. The way she hugged Sal, winked at her, was an assertion of her new role as Sal's confidante. Perhaps I've been fooling myself, but I had thought Sal and I were close. I had thought that here at last was something fragile that I was keeping together with stealth and tact.

Later Sal confirmed that she wants to spend more time with me and with Beth, by which I interpret, time when we are not just physically present for her, but mentally and imaginatively too. And she doesn't want to spend any time at all with Angie's twins. (I thought this was chancing her arm, as there is nothing much wrong with them – they're boisterous but – I'll let that pass.)

On the way home we stopped off at the Hi-Ho Cherry O educational toy shop and I bought a lump of clay. Sal was intrigued, curious to see what I'd do next. Back in Kalk Bay, I laid newspaper on the garden table and plonked the clay on top of it.

We're going to make a nativity scene, I said.

'But it's only August,' said Sal.

Some people make their Christmas cakes in January, I pointed out. We divided the clay into smaller lumps. Sal was still waiting for me to take the lead. I remembered reading somewhere that great sculptors actually see the shape they're going to make inside the clay, and just chip it out, remove its casing.

I'm going to start with Mary, I said. She'll be a basic triangle, like Claire. Sal smiled, a little doubtfully. I squeezed the clay into a cowled figure. Then I used a stick to start outlining an oval face and clasped hands. When it started to look recognisable, Sal stopped watching and started to mould her own piece of clay with evident pleasure.

'I'll make the baby,' she said and rolled a little sausage into a swaddled bundle. Together we made a crib that just exactly fitted its sleeping form. 'The little Lord Jesus, no crying he makes,' sang Sal, and then, more splendidly, 'Fall on your knees!'

Mrs Cloete came out to see what we were doing, and got caught up in the spirit of the moment. She made some damn fine beasts. Her donkey made Sal laugh out loud – her old fat laugh. Mrs Cloete took some fluff from Sir Nicholas's grooming brush to make a mane and tail. After two hours of intense creative work we had the entire cast – shepherds, cows, sheep, Joseph, an angel – drying in the sun.

Every time I was tempted to come up here and work or write to you, I stopped myself in mid-thought and found something else for us to do. Sir Nicholas was walked and groomed. I helped Sal with her elephant project (took a roll of expensive cardboard from Beth's office).

Sal sensed that things were going her way. 'Could we go back to that toy shop tomorrow? I saw something there I want to buy with my own money.'

I said yes, sure. But I found that I was grinding my teeth. There was this voice inside me whining, 'What about me?'

Sal didn't prevaricate at suppertime, though she didn't want anything that could be called a 'meal'. She did have a piece of salami with her dry roll, and a peeled minneola.

There is no note of love, no poem or yearning memory for you today, because I feel so jealous of you and, yes – resentful. It is just unfortunate that you and Theo seem to go on holidays, holidays, holidays while I struggle from month end to month end, hopping from one doomed ice floe to the next. Then I have started to think how, after all this, after hours and weeks and months, you might come to me in December or in March next year for just one half hour, even less, not even pausing long enough to sit down or slip your bag off your shoulder, for all I know with the engine of the Isuzu still running.

I feel almost overpowered by a sense of unmet needs. Forget all fancy words. I want a girlfriend. I want a lover. I want you. I know that by writing to you at all, I am accepting your rules, and that like a rebellious long-haired boy at a posh private school, I have no right to question the institution. If I want something else I must go, as Harry Botha-Reid used to say at Karoo Books when we balked at our drop in salaries, 'to another watering hole'.

I am losing faith. You say you love me, and you are manifestly good to me. All those books you've sent me; all the poems you've found inside me, and read and mulled over. The day I came home and found my broken, back-breaking chair had been replaced by a smart ergonomically designed one. The painting of the bay you bought to hang above my desk.

The painting. As we stripped it of its bubble wrap and hung it, Beth said something that I don't think she intended as hurtful. She said, 'Theresa's nice to everybody, isn't she?'

So, I shouldn't feel special, singled out. Perhaps I am merely another of your charity cases. I find this hard to believe. I know that when you read this you will rush to reassure me. Even I rush to reassure me. You expect more from me than your charity cases. You are really quite stern with me.

It's all wrong, isn't it? I should be older than you, and richer. But there are precedents. I think of Dorothea Brooke in *Middlemarch* and the feckless Will Ladislaw. I am Will Ladislaw with his sketchbook; you are Dorothea, full of money and good intentions. Only, Ladislaw had dash and charm. I need more dash.

Whoever heard of a thirty-seven-year-old white male driving a rusty Opel Kadett? Still living in the tumbledown house of his childhood? I should have one of those cars that feels as though it's moving on satin pillows, that hardly even whirrs as it glides. I should be living in a loft apartment with a slightly minimalist feel.

If you left Theo, packed a bag and drove here to me, how would we live? I've barely been able to support myself since leaving school eighteen years ago. You've said you have nothing to offer me – the truth is that I have nothing to offer you.

Except Chocolate Truffle Tart: *A velvet mousse tart made from double Belgian chocolate on a Pecan Nut crust. Served with a mixed Berry compote and topped with a sugar shard.*

Ask the chef for a velvet mousse tart
Whipped with dark Belgian, a real work of art.
The chocolate-y mousse in a pecan crust laid
And with it is served, now be not afraid
A berry compote that a poet would quote
And topped by the bard with a sweet sugar shard.

dum-diddy-dum-diddy-dum.

Tuesday 27th August
10.19 pm

I slept so well. Morning came as a surprise. I am rested. My

156

ears and throat feel fine. I'm not stiff. I had to stay with her till she was fast asleep, but Sal slept in her own bed.

This morning Sal promised to turn over a new leaf and eat when she's hungry. For breakfast she dipped a rusk into some tea, but afterwards wouldn't drink the tea because it had soggy lumps in it. I offered to strain it, of course.

Vera and Hannelie invited me to coffee and *pain au chocolat* at the Olympia. Vera and I arrived first. 'Can I ask you a personal question?' asked Vera while we waited. I looked doubtful, but she continued: 'Is there anything going on between you and Hannelie?' I was surprised. 'Harriet and Sal get on so well, I mean, and you're a single guy, aren't you?'

I said ye-es. You'll think I'm silly, but whenever people ask that, I hesitate, because in my heart, you are my soul's mate. It feels like a betrayal, a terrible denial, to say, 'I am single.' But of course I am. Ask anyone, ask Home Affairs.

Vera was enjoying the topic even if I wasn't. 'Well, I know she finds you attractive, because we've talked about it. She says she likes your Botticelli curls. Though I must say I don't think you'd suit her. Hannelie once told me she wants a man to overpower her, fell her and roll her onto a bed. I can't see you doing that, somehow.'

Thanks, I said. I was relieved when the arrival of Hannelie put an end to these speculations.

They wanted to hear about the psychologist. I was still feeling indignant at Claire's aspersions, so I'm afraid I raved a bit. As I spoke, I recognised a new unpleasant emotion: an unmistakable, unspeakable resentment towards Sal herself for bringing me to this impasse. How dare she harm herself, the little person we loved? But I couldn't say that aloud. We may not say aloud how we resent children. I concentrated instead on repeating what Claire had said, with my feelings footnoted. Vera and Hannelie, clearly both past masters at character assassination of complete strangers, encouraged me.

'Of course it's not your fault, how dare she imply that?' said Hannelie. 'What about Sal's real dad – whatshisname with the skinny wife – why didn't the psychologist dig into him, the Disney dad?'

I told them about Ron lying on his couch with his remote and his lottery ticket in his hand. That picture was symbolic of Ron's entire life, I said. It was because of people like Ron that Coke can holders in cars, on movie seats and deckchairs, had been invented. He was a slob and Lilian his wife who made Sal eat dry rye bread had dieted her brain to the size of a green jelly bean. ('Green, nogal,' said Hannelie.) I wanted very much to suggest that Ron and Lilian were to blame for Sal's anorexia. Or anyone else. Not me.

I am not concerned with rational thoughts. I want to kill someone. I want to find the one who started this: the school, lookist girls in Sal's class, advertising billboards, pop videos. Why, when there is so much evil being spread abroad, why do I – a man who loves size fourteen and sixteen women – have to get blamed? It became, as always, a poem:

Cecil Beaton is not dead enough
My niece is dieting to death:
it is time someone paid for the privilege.
'Who?' they asked me. I listed narrow minds
who conceived the fashion channel, wasted
writers of get-thin manuals, New York agencies
of brain diminishment and blood deficiencies,
editors and trimmers of all that nourishes, whoever

sells and draws fat profits from cellulite gels,
pop idols crammed into hungry, crying lyrics,
boys with funless stickers saying 'No fat chicks'
and all photographers and shadowy image men,
all the way back to Cecil Beaton. 'Cecil Beaton
is dead,' said Vera. That may be, I said,
but Cecil Beaton is not dead enough:
he must die again.

Vera and Hannelie were quite calmly accepting of my tirade.

As we were leaving, Hannelie asked if Sal and I would like to join her and Harriet at the Noordhoek Riding School tomorrow. Harriet wants to take up riding. 'Sal might like it, too,' said Hannelie. 'We're having a try-out.' I said it sounded like a good idea.

I have been carrying fury and irritation with me all day. When I was waiting at the pedestrian crossing outside school this afternoon, I pointed a warning finger at a car which went through on the amber light. Poet gets road rage.

Her teacher says Sal ate her lunch at school but then complained of a sore tummy. I hope it's just the much shrunken organ's response to getting food again. After school Sal and I went to the library together. The system didn't like my card or Sal's (they're from another branch, though technically all the city libraries have amalgamated). The large, amiable librarian just date-stamped the books and said 'Better in the head than on the shelf.' I couldn't believe it. What a relief after the prohibitory Land-of-No atmosphere that usually surrounds us.

Next we took Sir Nicholas for a walk on the Fish Hoek

sports fields that back onto the dunes. As we battled against the wind, the following dialogue took place: SAL: John, do you like fish? JOHN: Yes, I love fish. SAL: You can get them at the Blue Route mall for R7. JOHN: Really? What kind of fish? A snoek? SAL: There's different kinds. A little purple one, a see-through one, a catfish. JOHN: Oh, pet fish! SAL: Will you let me have one? You said you love fish.

So tomorrow I'm buying an inedible fish. At least it has made her forget about the toy shop visit.

There was a soccer game in progress on the field and its perimeter was crowded with other people walking their dogs. For safety's sake, we headed Sir Nicholas the small-dog-eater off towards the river and walked on the dirt track beside it. He pretended to be interested in butterflies on the bank but was really just edging nearer and nearer the water for a good muddy splash.

Sal brought out a scrumpled piece of foolscap from her pocket. It was a love-letter from a boy in her class, bad Noah in fact. It goes something like this: 'Sal I love you. I will do anything for you. Do you love me? Say yes or no. If you do not love me I won't do anything for you.'

I said that's a classic love poem in the Renaissance tradition. 'What's the Renaissance?' asked Sal. She knows about Shakespeare, but I told her about Sydney, Spenser and Donne. Donne was much better, I said, than the others. They just say the usual things, you know – your teeth are like pearls and there are roses in your cheeks and oh I'm suffering. But Donne's got this love poem to his girlfriend, urging her to take her clothes off. It's like a high-class striptease. When she gets down to the last layer, he suddenly pulls off his nightshirt and is naked before her, even though she's spent 46 lines undressing.

Then he quips, *What needst thou have more covering than a man.* You get it? Covering – clothes – him covering her?

'Oh, gross,' said Sal.

What are you going to reply, I asked.

'I'm going to say: Dear Noah, I LIKE you. Don't try anything funny with me.'

I felt relieved because I really don't approve of this Noah boy. I think he's being brought up in a bar. One morning I was helping Sal bring a project of hers into the classroom before school. As she unpacked her books and tidied her desk, I watched Noah and his mates in the back row. Noah had punched two holes into a tin of condensed milk. He drank and then offered the tin to his friend, saying, 'Do you want to suck my semen?' I don't think Sal heard. I'm pretty sure she didn't, and probably wouldn't know what the word meant anyway. But Noah caught my eye and smirked. He wanted to see whether the only adult in the room would chastise him. The whole pain of his life flashed before me. How he would struggle to find love and, struggling, turn to hate. I looked at him coldly, with the merest sneer around my mouth and nostrils. Then I looked away, as if he was not interesting to me.

I don't know whether other adults also try to bring up children using facial expressions.

After our walk on the field, on the way home, we stopped at the harbour. Talk of fish had reminded me of how I used to love fish-cakes as a child, and I wanted to make some for supper. For the mixture I used a little freshly steamed hake and a tin of mackerel. The main thing is to have the fish-cakes with a really delicious homemade garlic mayonnaise. I think Sal agreed to a fish-cake because it was a way of eating the aioli.

161

I've just finished a brilliant biography of Gertrude Stein by a woman called Diana Souhami. Tonight I'll start *The Surgeon of Crowthorne* by Simon Winchester. I feel insecure when I don't know what I'm going to read next.

I am sorry about my despairing tone yesterday. They say that despair is the worst sin, the sin against the Holy Ghost.

Wednesday 28th August
9.16 pm

Beth is back! Sal and I drove to the airport this evening to fetch her. She came on a domestic flight from Johannesburg so we didn't have to wait for her to clear customs. When Sal caught sight of her mother she let out a little sigh, as if she'd been holding her breath, as if until that moment she hadn't quite believed that Beth would return. I saw Beth take in Sal's thinner frame, run her hands down it before embracing her tightly.

I roasted a chicken for supper. Sal had one drumstick, with the skin peeled off. She picked the bits of salad she liked out of the bowl and refused the potatoes. I said nothing, but offered a piece of bread. She hesitated, but accepted it, eating only the soft inside part, with no butter.

Just now, when Sal was in the bath, Beth thanked me and said, 'You must have gone through hell.' I said I didn't think I deserved her thanks. Beth insisted, said Sal had told her about the horses and the fish.

The horses and the fish, oh yes. This morning I drove

to the Blue Route Centre to buy a goldfish from the pet shop. They gave it to me in a plastic bag. The bowl and gravel were more expensive than the mere R7 Sal had mentioned in her petition. At home, decanting the fish into its bowl, I spoke aloud. I said, I am not even very good at looking after people, fish. You may not, in fact, be a lucky fish.

Then later, Hannelie and I drove together to Noordhoek with the two little girls. We were all bundled up in coats and thick jackets because the wind was bitterly cold. It is a lovely riding school, with acres of green fields, trees, a stream, sandy tracks leading off to the beach, paddocks with horses being lunged or schooled or just going about their horsey lives. The horses are stabled not in old-fashioned rows, but under a single roof in a huge square complex with fenced off sections and a central aisle that you walk through, your hair being gently tested for edibility by the muzzles above you. Hannelie and I watched while Harriet and Sal were helped onto ponies. Then we wandered around the paddocks while they were gently led around a ring with a group of beginners. Sal rode a pony called Flare which was apparently very well behaved. She sang its praises all the way home, intermittently criticising a girl called Jade who'd ignored the instructor and said 'When can we canter?' while rattling a gate impatiently. Sal said she was holding thumbs her mother would let her take lessons.

'I think it's a brilliant idea,' said Beth. 'I'm keen for her to have lessons, though they do seem expensive. They say you just have to get an unhappy girl to fall in love with a horse and your problems are solved.'

I said I haven't solved the problem and, worse still, I think I may have contributed to it in some way. After all, she stopped eating while under my care. Sal continues to limit her food intake, and to complain of tummy aches at school. Sometimes she sinks into long silent sadnesses. She's herself part of the time, but also sometimes seems to drift from me.

I said that today after school I'd asked her to tell me her latest worries. I say 'latest' because they are always like breaking news. Sal told me that she is scared of growing up and not being called smidgen any more, of going to Grade 4, of ever going to the twins' house, of having to go on a long holiday with her dad, of me and you getting old and frail.

But your dad's never mentioned taking you away for a long holiday, I had said to Sal.

'But it happens to other children,' said Sal.

'And Beth and I are still quite young. Your mom's only just turning forty.'

'I know but didn't you say the other day that you think you might need glasses? You're just going to get weaker and frailer and then you'll die.'

I assured her that I was not going to die of long-sightedness.

Listening to her anxieties and trying to respond to them, I feel perplexed. How do we make other people happy?

Beth considered the question. She said she didn't know, but she'd try to spend more time with Sal for a start.

If you spend more time with her, you'll have to cut down on the work, and then what about money, I said. I saw the worry on Beth's face and immediately felt bad. Look, I said, I'm getting some extra money writing doggerel. We could use it to fix the cracks. I'm sure I can pack more in my day. I could take on some ordinary editing work too – you know, the usual marketing and management books. I think I've been a bit profligate with my time until now.

It's true. Ironically, on the day my sister returns, I discover the knack to life as surrogate mother and multitasker. I find that if I keep moving, if I all but eliminate naps, newspaper reading, coffee shop outings, friendly chats to Red on the phone, and if I move very rapidly from task to task, I can just fit everything into the day. Sal's lunch box, uniform, homework, waking, reading, consolation, going to sleep, tea, breakfast, after-school activities take up a large chunk of the day. Then there's Sir Nicholas's exercise, food and excrement removal. Then clean house, cook, laundry, shop, empty bins, recycle. Personal hygiene. Rush to my post as editor of *The Unofficial View*: process new submissions, write rejections, feel anxious. Swap to restaurant menu: find rhymes for 'tomato' and 'aubergine', feel slightly defiled. Entertain the daily visits of Tiny the bergie and Mrs Cloete. Now all these domestic duties are about to be halved, at least.

Thursday 29th August
9.22 pm

It's actually happened. I can't believe it. Ron won the lottery. Not the top, top amount but about R115 000. He matched five numbers in the midweek draw. He came around here early, crowing. I've never seen Ron so animated. He really felt as though he personally had achieved something.

We all sat around the kitchen table congratulating him.

Beth was still in her dressing gown, but Sal was smart in her school uniform. Ron in his suit of course. I couldn't work out why he'd driven all the way to Kalk Bay from Newlands. Surely he should be celebrating with Lilian?

'I'm giving you some money, Liz,' he said. 'Not everything,' he added hastily, 'but I'd like you to have R28000.' He's the only person in the world who calls Beth 'Liz'.

'Oh, no,' she said. 'You must keep it, Ron.'

I nearly fell over, as the expression goes. I'm pleased to say that Ron persisted.

'No, Liz, I've thought about this, it's what I've always told myself I would do if I won. This place of yours is a bit run down, I know. Maybe you'd like to do something in terms of that. I mean, it's where Sal lives, and you might, for example, like to fix it up a bit. Or maybe you could get a char every now and then. It'd give you more time for whatever.'

I was nervous that Beth might find some high-minded reason to turn Ron down, so I was standing by to intervene if necessary.

But Beth was very mild, very grateful.

'It's very good of you, Ron, extremely generous. Have you spoken to Lilian about this?'

'Well, I'm giving her the rest to do whatever she likes with. She can buy clothes or beauty products if she likes. So she can't complain.'

I said: Ron, I don't understand. You've been wanting to win the lottery for so long. Surely that's because you wanted the money for yourself?

'No,' said Ron. 'I just wanted to show everyone I could do it. Now I've proved it to you.'

It made me think how, all those Saturdays and Wednesdays

when Ron looked like he was just lying on his sofa with his lottery ticket and his remote, he was actually doing something.

'Well, thank you again, Ron,' said Beth, 'because to tell you the truth the house has been worrying me.'

'And it's an asset,' said Ron. 'You could get a nice clean new house on a golf estate for what they're charging around here these days.'

Ron brought out his calculator and worked out our sums. R28 000 for just over half the repairs as per Axel's quote, the rest to be raised as a loan against the house. Less R1 780 for my menu rhymes.

And Beth might get another really big project, I said.

'Yes,' said Beth, 'there's a lot of movement in the property world around here, as you pointed out. I might get a really big contract.'

It's a longstanding habit of ours to live off imagined future earnings.

'Well, we can't factor in your wishful thinking,' said Ron. 'That's bad accounting practice.'

I remembered the Mars Bars bought and the Mars Bars sold. A debit in one column is a credit in another.

'I'll give up ballet,' said Sal. 'Will that help?'

Ron pretended to punch some more numbers in. 'Perfect,' he said. 'That tips the balance.' Though we both knew riding would cost about twice the ballet fees.

I've said terrible things about Ron, I know, and it's too late now to go back and say, Wait – he's a great guy. Because everybody would know that I'm just saying that because of the money. Ron is like the Lakeside bakery. No one notices its pretty gable and unusually tall façade, everyone just drives past it. One day some developer-prince is going to buy that bakery, renovate its frontage and turn it into something. Then it will be too late to say, 'I always thought it had potential.' It will have left us behind, sweeping off on rich arms.

What I've said about Ron, the picture I've painted of him to people, reminds me of the horrible moral tale Father Nolan taught us before our first confession. There was once a woman who was a terrible gossip. She spread stories far and wide. One day she felt remorse. Dreading her penance, she nevertheless confessed. The priest said that her penance was to take a pillow out to a windy spot, cut it open and allow the feathers to disperse. Then she should report back to him. This she did. 'Now those feathers,' said the priest, 'are the slanders you've spread. Go and collect all the feathers and put them back in the pillow case.' After a week, the woman returned to the priest and admitted defeat. The priest said, 'Then how can I forgive you?'

At this point I find myself like a person who has started to tell a joke but has forgotten the punchline. What could be the possible point of it? See how great God's mercy is? Go and do not sin again? I hate stories with morals. Isn't there at least a possibility of getting away scot-free?

Friday 30th August
5.55 pm

Early this morning I took Sir Nicholas on a difficult walk up the steep, sharply zigzagging ravine path that skirts the cliff face above St James. Reaching the top panting, he lapped water from the natural bowls formed in the rocks. Already, spring flowers are carpeting the plateau.

I thought how in a few months' time this walk will be uncomfortably hot and exposed, but today it was just perfect. Down below us, the bay lay serene. People were at work, but not me. I walk free.

It was after ten when we descended, and the first thing I saw as we came down through the old cemetery into Quarterdeck Road was Ryno's 4x4 right up on the pavement. Picking up his owner's scent, Sir Nicholas raced up the alley at the side of the house to the open back door and straight into Ryno's big, black leather-clad arms.

Dog's gone:

doggone.

Mrs Cloete was beaming to see her son home and well, though shaking her head about the dangers he exposes himself to.

'They murder people in the Eastern Cape, you know, it's frontier country,' she said.

'That's why I carry this,' said Ryno, patting a large hardbound bird guide. We looked puzzled. Then Ryno opened the book. A square had been neatly hollowed out, and inside the hole lay a revolver. He says he keeps the book lying casually next to him on the passenger seat at all times.

'Two things your hijacker doesn't do: read or swim. That's why if I ever get hijacked, I'm going to drive straight into the nearest body of water.'

Ryno showed us his Transkei photographs – women with babies strapped to their backs gathering shellfish at low tide on deserted beaches, pristine mangrove islands, wild white men, piratical and castaway in appearance, drinking on the wooden decks of their illegal bungalows, queues of pensioners at an unchanged general dealer's, boy goat-herders, grandmothers with pipes, people walking impossible distances to vestigial settlements.

Then he greeted his mother, whistled for Sir Nicholas, and departed for his house in Noordhoek. He promises to join us this evening at Ferdinand's restaurant where I am launching the menu and also reading some real poetry. For money, I stress. Plus, Ferdinand has generously offered to feed my family and friends for free.

When Ryno had gone, Mrs Cloete returned to her cottage and Beth to her office, I was at last able to make myself a cup of hot chocolate. It's the sort of drink you have to make for yourself. Once you start offering it to everyone else it loses its decadence. I always make it in a particular dark blue mug, and deliberately leave some of the chocolate lumps undissolved, floating richly in the foam. I have it with anchovy toast. No restaurant can ever match the bespoke meals we make for ourselves.

Later Mrs Cloete came in to ask for the addresses of Tizzy Clack and Primrose Mkhaliphi, of the Good Samaritan poem. Why do you want their addresses, I asked.

'Well,' said Mrs Cloete, 'I'd like to write to them and tell them how I enjoyed their poems.'

I gave her the addresses, trying to imagine their responses. Poets don't get a lot of fan mail. When Sal came home from school, I heard Mrs Cloete summoning her. I saw Sal emerge from the cottage looking very important, holding two envelopes. We are no longer being asked to search for the jack of diamonds.

I have this sense of possible happiness all around me. I get definite glimpses of happiness and peace. Last night, going out in the rain to Fish Hoek with Sal to buy my favourite seafood pizza – the inside of the Italian restaurant was so cosy, every available space draped in soccer flags or plastered with old newspaper cuttings featuring the fat proprietor's much younger face, when he was a football star in Naples. Now he toils in his vest over the glowing pizza oven. Rough men ('I've been a bum in Mozambique') perched on bar stools offered me a glass of red wine while we waited, called for a Coke for Sal (she drank it). The real Italian mama brought in steaming bowls of pasta for her regulars – a thin man with his girlfriend, who said I'd have to watch Sal when she got older, she already had the look. I thought how these vignettes of life, of people just carrying on and getting their little tiny bits of satisfaction, are what I want. It was a dark night, and inside was this bright, bright scene. There must be many others like that. I need to unglue myself from this computer from time to time and go out there and take pleasure from other people's lives.

Sal had been planning not to eat, but the strong smell of garlic, and I think the picture-book look of the place, made her change her mind. She'd have a small margarita, but she wouldn't be able to finish it, she said. That's fine, I said, perhaps your mother would like a piece.

Axel the builder came round today. I hadn't realised it when I contacted him, but apparently he and Beth have worked together before. They had a long and mutually enjoyable conversation about guttering and damp-proofing.

It's my debut as a commercial poet this evening – the big party at Ferdinand's.

Saturday 31st August
6.20 pm

Reading the menu doggerel last night at the opening

of Ferdinand's restaurant was like being someone else altogether. I looked deep inside myself and found a different John – jaunty, extrovert. He stood at the mike and smiled with throwaway charm. He read a new poem, suitably raunchy/funny for the occasion, and felt like the Mr Delivery of the poetry world:

Spam
I'm being spammed by a man of American genus –
wants to add three inches to my asterisk penis.
'She'll love it,' my spam-man says:
'Suddenly satisfy her, blast her to Venus.'
A female impaled on my chimerical penis.

Who's 'she'? Who's 'her'?
Do you think, Mr Spam man, her's like Pasiphae
has to mate with a bull before she's satisfied?
Though I'm sure *her* wasn't begging for more
when delivered of the minotaur.

Mr Spam man with your battering ram –
like everyone who sells crap
you don't care what people really need.
You can't sell a man longer
words to reach deep inside of her,
words with more girth
to touch her inner core –
'con amore', 'je t'adore',
 'you remind me of the fertile fields of Kenya'.

The things she wants, I could give her for free
a salty afternoon next to the slow distant sea;
a longer than usual kiss: 'I miss you, I miss you.'
More and more and more of this: more softness.

They laughed. I felt strange. Because although the poem reflects my thoughts, it isn't one I'd have written if I hadn't visualised the audience beforehand, thought about what they'd like. I fear this crowd-pleasing side of me.

Of course when my reading was over, I drank too much out of relief. I sat down at our table and actually gulped my glass of wine down. I noticed that Ryno, who was sitting next to Hannelie, kept having to stretch his arm out along the back of her chair, as if there wasn't enough room for him. Hannelie reached across to me and touched my hand.

'You were wonderful, John. You had me in tears.'

Hannelie, I said, you're always in tears.

Sal had a taste of Beth's lobster bisque and liked it so much Ferdinand insisted she should have a bowl of her own. I think Ferdinand was quite charmed by Beth's effusive praise. Mrs Cloete would only eat a starter, but Ryno more than made up for his mother's bird-like appetite. I felt compelled to eat the dishes I'd composed rhymes about, and Ryno helped me out, pretending that everything tasted nicer because of my poetic advertising. He composed his own witty verses at which we were supposed to laugh: 'Here's a fish: what a dish!' Occasionally, other diners would come up and congratulate me. Then Ryno, who'd started off with a couple of brandies in the bar and had called for our second bottle of red wine, would stick his head into the conversation and say something like, 'I'm his friend, you know. I'm the poet's buddy,' and reminisce about our school days.

Today I woke up with a sore head but I've taken a lot of Prohep and Disprin. I walked with Sal while she rode her bike round the Clovelly estuary, and we spoke briefly about her second visit to Claire the psychologist, on Monday afternoon.

'I just don't feel like opening up any more,' she said, with a sophisticated sigh.

Then tell her that, I said.

I came home and had a nap. Poets need their sleep, and anyway I have to go out again this evening.

Tomorrow you'll be there, Theresa, and you'll reply. Then everything will be all right again until December, when once again my letters will dangle in the cyber air.

You are away again. You and Theo have these things called holidays. Then you don't write at all. These gaps are worse for me than the occasional hiatus caused by a cyber backlog, because they arouse my envy. Why is Theo allowed to be alone with you in beautiful settings? Why is Theo with you at all, when it is me whom you love? But what if you were here, with me in this very room? Would I know who I was? Would I write? And I wonder too, if I am not compelled by you because I can't 'have' you. I would hate to end up in a house with a picket fence and a woman to whom I belonged and to whom I would, out of love, defer, giving up little things until at last I would forget my true self and fade from view. Little things like silence, like a solitary cup of coffee in the sunrise of a sleepless night, like humble suppers of toast and leftovers eaten standing up, like meetings, with friends who just happen to be women, like unaccompanied swims and walks, like the habits of poetry and reading. You would not call for these sacrifices, though I would freely make them for you. Even if we shared meals, beds and holidays, it would still be with a slight sense of surprise at the felicity of one another's company.

I'm glad at least that you are by the sea, though I imagine Hermanus must be like Kalk Bay at this time of the year. I can see Hangklip from our front window, but not Hermanus. Another holiday for Theresa. But I don't resent it, I don't. I mean, I mustn't.

You certainly deserve a rest. I don't know how you've kept your patience with this Frikkie business. I understand your giving him the first wheelchair, when he was being

175

pushed around in a purloined supermarket trolley. Then I kind of understand why you agreed to upgrade it to a model more suited to farm roads. But now my beloved Theresa is investigating the possibility of a Paralympic standard wheelchair. Then I suppose that since Frikkie does have aspirations in this regard, you will seek out training for him.

There are so few people like you in the world. I can't believe that someone as good as you loves someone as venal as me.

Another still, hot day dawned, buzzing with the high expectations of school holidays. This morning I took Sal, Harriet and Vera's Alan along with me when I went down for my swim at Dalebrook pool. Alan so loved it he stood before me, shivering and thin in his towel, asking could we stay there all day, could we come again tomorrow? I felt bad reminding him that his father the plagiarist was fetching him for the night. On the slippery back wall of the tidal pool, Sal fights with him (hand to hand combat) but then steps back in her little Speedo costume and says, 'I'm the princess, I don't fight. I wear pretty clothes and write poetry.' Alan was mesmerised by this performance; Sal took advantage of the lull to dive in and swim to Harriet on the rock island.

When we got back here, we found Axel sanding the kitchen dresser. Beth sliced watermelon for the children and told them to eat it in the garden.

'I suspect this is yellowwood underneath all the layers of paint,' said Axel.

'Looks like it was even painted blue once,' said Beth.

Fearing an invoice, I said, Axel, you don't have a mandate for that scraping.

He said solidly, 'I want to do it.'

Still in my damp swimming costume, wrapped only in a faded kikoi, I came up here to work and to check my mail, though without the anticipation I feel when you are there. I mustn't enquire whether it would not be possible for you to send me a brief daily text message during these compulsory vacations, or to find some way of contacting me. A Christmas greeting at least, a Happy New Year?

But there was good news, at least. A mail from Hector Newbury, the oldest member of Red's poetry group, the one I met in September, attaching the poem I'd requested. He's eighty-seven, he says, but all hooked up to the internet. At Red's poetry evening, when I heard Hector read his epic poem 'Five Farms From Here' I was impressed by the magnificent beauty and plainness of its design. I was also moved by the way Hector intermittently dabbed his eyes with his handkerchief. When I mentioned this to him afterwards, he laughed heartily and dabbed his eyes some more. 'They water all the time now,' he said. 'Even my tears are fleeing this sinking ship.'

Speaking of tears, Hannelie arrived in a state to fetch Harriet. We were having tea in the kitchen when she burst in, her mouth quivering, breath shaken and uneven. Axel took one look at her and immediately found an urgent need to rummage through his tool-box in the safety of the backyard.

'What's wrong, Hannelie, tell us?' asked Beth.

She told us her story. Walking across the car park outside Fish Hoek library with some members of her book club, Hannelie had listened while the women complained about their husbands. 'But I'd never get divorced,' said one, 'because no one invites a divorced woman to their dinner parties.' A raised set of eyebrows and meaningful looks and nudges prompted the witless woman to add, 'I don't mean someone like you, Hannelie, because you're such fun. And such an asset, the way you always wash up afterwards and play with the children.'

Hannelie sobbed as she retold the story. 'The worst thing is, it's true,' she said.

Beth was outraged. 'What kind of a book club do you belong to, Hannelie? They sound completely illiterate!'

We only have one pretty cup and matching saucer, but I made Hannelie's tea in it.

'This time of year really gets to me,' said Hannelie, in a wet, broken voice.

Beth and I exchanged a glance.

'I know what we'll do,' said Beth. 'We'll have our own parties this Christmas season and especially not invite any married people.'

Could we make an exception for Red and Frances, I asked.

'All right,' said Beth, 'but there must be no more marriages.'

I couldn't agree more.

In the evening, Beth, Sal and I packed a picnic and went down to the park for the annual Kalk Bay community party. Ryno and his mom joined us; he brought a fold-out camp chair for her. Mrs Cloete was in high spirits because in this one eventful day she'd received a letter and a phonecall, from two different people, both poets. She was no longer an invisible old lady, without a newsworthy contribution to the conversation. Primrose Mkhaliphi had sent a long letter, thanking Mrs Cloete for praising her poem and attaching another one for her consideration. And earlier, Mrs Cloete had a phonecall from Tizzy Clack, inviting her out for coffee. She's been in regular correspondence with them since August. Throughout the fourth term, when I dropped Sal at school, she'd stop off first at the postbox and drop in Mrs Cloete's thick letters, addressed in an old lady elegant scrawl. When did Sal start to make me drop her rather than escort her to the classroom? When did she start eating egg mayonnaise sandwiches? *All change, all change*, as Tizzy's poem says.

Sitting on the grassy slope with a beer and my closest companions, watching the local women show off their belly-dancing prowess, I felt very cheerful. It didn't even seem to matter that one of the featured acts, a strange Saartje Baartman creature on stilts, was making all the Kalk Bay babies cry.

I fell to reflecting on the problem of Hannelie, and wondered aloud whether Axel might do for her.

Maybe we could subtly find out whether she has any little things that need doing around her house, I said. Then we could send Axel along to fix them.

Beth was unimpressed with my idea. 'Don't try to be a matchmaker,' she advised.

Ryno agreed with her.

I'm really taken with Axel's name, I said. It makes ours seem so frivolous. We should all be called after stout, useful things: Trowel, Spade, Nail, Grouting.

Except you, my saint. Oh, yes, I meant to say that Sal is delighted with the advent calendar you sent. Thank you, beloved unbeliever.

Sal's excited about Christmas; I too am full of anticipation. It's twelve days to go before the special launch of *The Unofficial View* #24. It's true that particular issues of poetry journals don't usually get launched, but Mrs Feinstein believed in marketing and publicity, so there's a modest budget set aside for the purpose. Just a little party and some reading.

I'm sure I was supposed to get quotes for the printing

costs, but Red Moffat's had a lot of experience – his poetry group put out a collection every quarter and so Red has 'a little man' in Claremont who prints and does a simple stapling job from his home. I need to get the manuscript to him soon, before the end of the week. The cover is a beautiful abstract doodle by Beth. Ryno is organising a basic stage, mike and sound system. Hannelie is going to bring the wine and the hired glasses because I'm doing the snacks. I feel completely fine about nepotism. I think we may be genetically wired for it.

Wednesday 18th December
11.15 pm

This morning's swim was made difficult by the waves crashing over the wall, bringing in great slippery bodies of seaweed and nearly pushing me up against the rock in the centre of the pool. Alone again. But all along the pavement on my way there, I pass dog-walkers with straining leashes, and I think always of you. As you must think of me whenever you see lonely poets working in quiet rooms.

In my quiet room this morning I received an email from the secretary of the Feinstein Trust enquiring how my editing of *The Unofficial View* was getting along. She put 'editing' in inverted commas. I get very nervous about inverted commas around individual words. They imply such a profound doubt. How is my 'editing' going? I think it's nearly complete, if I add the contribution I received today from Catherine Magwaza.

I discovered Catherine in October, when I was canvassing poetry collectives and slam poetry events. I recorded one of her poems, transcribed it and then sent it back to her to check. At last today she's written giving permission to publish it:

With respect
Regrettably you have eaten the peanut butter
    sandwiches
intended for starving children who walk to school
drowsy for lack of food
Though perhaps you thought this was good,
There has been a change of regime
I'm afraid that concomitantly you must report to
Ellis Park for a mass vomiting.

Lamentably you have built yourself a very large
    mansion
with bricks intended for those who sleep wrapped in
    plastic
Though perhaps you think that's fantastic,
There has in fact been a change of regime and
I'm afraid you must report to Ellis Park
for a mass vomiting and emetic.

Alas, you have squandered the cash budget
intended for HIV treatment action
Though perhaps that gave you satisfaction
I must point out there has been a change of regime
I'm afraid you must report to Ellis Park asap
and donate all your blood to charity.

I'd still like one more poem for the edition, but I've run out of time. Feeling gruesomely efficient, I decided on a final running order, finished my introduction and drove in the sweltering heat of midday to Claremont to drop the manuscript and disk with Red's printer. You can see from the chaos in this study that I've been busy.

When I returned, I ate two nectarines while leaning over the sink. Then I coached Sal in remedial maths. She's been promoted to Grade Four on condition she does some extra work on numeracy during the holidays. Nobody fails any more; parents are euphemistically informed that 'the learner has only partially fulfilled the requirements at this level'.

Sal and I got stuck into measurement and shape. Sal has no difficulty naming all the geometric shapes; in fact she rather relishes them: trapezium, kite, rhombus, parallelogram. But story sums are hard work, because she gets too caught up in the narrative element. One sum began, 'If Dad does two hours of exercise every day of the week ...' I was reading it slowly, hoping it would make sense to her, but Sal finished the sentence with '... I'd be surprised.' This is not a cartoon strip, I said, this is real life.

Next, we did time. In helping her, I briefly lost my temper over twenty to, quarter to etc. I was wielding an old broom handle in order to point out things on the kitchen clock. When Sal kept saying five to was five past or twenty to was eight something, I banged the broomstick on the floor and its remaining plastic bits went flying. Axel, sanding the kitchen dresser again, kept silently at his work, though his silence was a comment in itself. Meanwhile, Sal seems to find my histrionics quite funny. Doubtless she'll use them later in life when she's interpreting Ladies Macbeth and Bracknell.

'Let me make you some tea,' she said at last. 'I can see you're taking strain.'

I calmed down by making a vegetable curry for supper. The recipe comes from a pioneer-era cookbook:

the endpapers have a cosy illustration of a firelit laager scene. It even has an appendix with recipes for ostrich soap ('wonderful for hair shampooing') and a cure for 'Colic in a Horse'. It's comforting to know that we have this information, should the need ever arise, in an uncertain future, to make our own soap or to treat a colicky horse. I knew Sal wouldn't touch a vegetable curry so I tossed some strips of chicken fillet in a mixture of oil, onions, cumin and curry powder: Hannelie's trick.

Beth felt the need for some exercise after supper, so we walked, the three of us, along Boyes Drive as far as the view site above Bailey's grave. It is so high there, higher than our slope in Kalk Bay. Below us, Sunrise beach stretched away in an unbroken ribbon of inviting sand. Ryno and I wanted to walk its full length when we were boys, all the way to Gordon's Bay, but the Defence Force had blocked off part of it. After Gordon's Bay the coastline becomes rocky, though interspersed with beaches. I could scramble along there till I reached your side.

I'm showered and ready for bed now, utterly exhausted. That's the only way to do it these stifling summer nights: lie down under a sheet or thin cotton blanket and fall asleep immediately without tossing, with a light breeze just teasing the curtain.

Thursday 19th December
8.45 pm

There was no water in either Dalebrook or St James pool for a swim this morning – I'd forgotten to check from the top window – so I jogged back home, fetched my car keys and drove to Fish Hoek. I swim there at least once a week, usually because the tidal pool here is empty of water or too full of people. The men who swim at Fish Hoek corner in the morning are very interested in the water temperature: '16.9', they like to say, heartily, reading from a thermometer pendant. The women just stride in, adjusting their bathing caps and laughing as they catch waves on their boogie boards. I'm sort of friendly to them, but quite relieved once I've passed the breakers and am alone.

I thought today about those few seconds before you're properly 'in' cold water: how unpleasant it feels as you stand there clutching your unwilling sides. It must be fear of the evolutionary step backwards: back to the old amphibian life. Then, when you're in, how lovely it is, all cares gone.

When I got back here, Harriet and Sal were in the garden trying to coax a tired rock pigeon into a shoebox. The bird was not bleeding, but could not fly.

'My mom's got an empty bird cage,' said Harriet. 'I'll phone her and tell her to bring it.'

They were at the top of the steps when Sal called out, 'Oh, yes, John, a woman dropped off something for you in the letterbox.'

I lifted the wooden lid and found a letter from Barbara Daniel. I met her last month when I accompanied Ryno on a photographic assignment for the TAC. Her daughter had just died of an AIDS-related illness. While Ryno tried to capture her on film, I chatted to her. She wasn't one of those people who sit back and wait to be interviewed. Instead, she asked me lots of questions, and I found myself talking to her about poetry, even showing her a few poetry journals I had lying in my car. I felt like an evangelist, but she listened and asked for my address. 'I might write something,' she said. 'I haven't finished saying what I want to say.'

I stood there today at the postbox, holding in my hand what she still wanted to say:

Van 'n gewone ma aan die Minister van Gesondheid
Ek sê dankie vir die raad
maar op die ou end
het die knoffel gefaal
en olyfolie niks behaal
om VIGS
te verweer
of haar skrale lyf
weer
te laat
leef.

Was daar tog niks
wat ons nog kon doen –

ons twee –
u, die hoof
van die hooggeplaastes,
en ek,
die naaste
van haar naasbestaandes,
van een vlees
en nou
die seerste beroof?

It had to come from a first-time writer.

I rushed up here and phoned the printers. Much to the chagrin of the little man Red had recommended, I recalled the manuscript of *The Unofficial View*, just as it was about to go to press.

'Any minute now it's Christmas,' he said. 'I'm not printing over Christmas.'

Give me a day, I said, one day to adjust the manuscript.

There must be a scientific theory to explain mad, last-minute rushes – why they are obligatory.

Hannelie popped her head around the door to greet me when she came to collect Harriet. She was carrying an elaborate Taj Mahal-style bamboo cage.

'It's for Mrs Gray,' she said.

Who's Mrs Gray, I asked, but kept my eyes on the screen.

'The rock pigeon the little girls are saving,' she said. She hovered for a while, but I didn't want to lose my train of thought so I said nothing. Hannelie slipped away, leaving behind a faint scent of sandalwood.

When I went downstairs eventually, in search of a drink and something to eat, I saw Sal standing next to Axel as he peered into the cage.

'I think she might make it,' he said gruffly.

He'd brought some wild bird seed.

It's nice having Axel here, fixing things. Today he sawed out the rotten floorboards upstairs. We now have an interesting hole (waiting for beams and new boards). When I'm downstairs, I can hear the 'psshh' of Beth's steam iron and she can hear Sal 'teaching' Harriet in their game of school-school. For Sal, the antonym of 'fresh' is 'vrot', and soldiers are 'armed to their toes'.

I finished my revision of *The Unofficial View*, so it's ready to go back to the printer tomorrow. Then after all these hours spent with other people's work, I felt a yearning to escape into a poem of my own making, to carve out a little private retreat. I remembered one stolen evening of ours, and I wrote:

Hibiscus Kiss
Still thrilled by your kiss
behind the secret hibiscus
on a bench made of living branches
under the still
open
starry
sky.

(Still waiting for the next one,
like a wave break
on the reef beyond
the hibiscus kiss.)

Friday 20th December
10.55 pm

I swam earlier than usual this morning. Even so, there are others who have the same idea about avoiding the crowds. When I came back, starving, I found that Beth had made muffins. I had about six, by which I mean three, with jam and cream.

There was a tentative knock on the front door, not Tiny's come-out-you-infidels hammering. It was someone from my swelling company of little-liked people: Tizzy Clack. Since their correspondence began, she's come more than once to take Mrs Cloete out to coffee. The first

187

time she visited, I hid behind the curtain up here and peeped down at them. But this morning, the alleyway that leads down to Mrs Cloete's cottage was locked, so Tizzy Clack knocked on our door and I've had to meet her at last. I steeled myself, told myself to be nice and then she would be nice. Which is just what happened. She even said what an honour it was to be published by me. By me, me, me. She kissed me on the cheek. I am on kissing terms with Tizzy Clack.

I drove to Claremont to drop off the manuscript and disk with the disgruntled printer. He works from home and he must be very busy because his garden is a forlorn patch of dry, weed-infested kikuyu and his entrance hall almost completely blocked by towers of shrink-wrapped publications. I felt bad about leaving my poets with this Rumpelstiltskin character, but there was no alternative.

The traffic on the way home was backed up from the Blue Route intersection. Everyone was heading down to the coast for a swim. I watched my temperature gauge nervously, but it stayed steady at the halfway mark. There was even a traffic jam on Boyes Drive. Eventually, I pulled over onto the pavement under a flowering gum and left the Opel there, making my way home on foot.

I've spent the afternoon feeling jealous of John Milton. It is Mrs Cloete's fault. She complained that her eyesight is failing (couldn't read the menu while out with Tizzy) and suddenly remembered a poem that began: *When I consider how my light is spent* ... Which poem was it from, she wanted to know. I found Milton's sonnet for her and helped her understand the tricky bits in the octave. She's gone off happily, probably to make notes for her correspondents. But now Milton's sonnet is stuck in my head, the way he so perfectly captures both the artist's plaintive egotism and, in a stunning switch to the wide-angled, aerial view, the utter inconsequence of the individual.

At about five, I took Sal Christmas shopping in the village. She wanted to buy her mother a present. Unluckily, we encountered Angie and the twins in a crowded gift shop.

'Hello, dwarf,' they said, and tried to pick Sal up.

I was about to intervene, when Sal adopted an almost karate-like pose and said, 'Talk to my hand.'

Undeterred, the twins started to needle her on her report card.

'So did you pass? What did you get for English? Brilliant! And maths? Oh, shame, Sal, we got fives for everything! Did you really do so badly in maths? You'll probably have to go to dreadful Dotty for extra lessons!'

'See the concern in my eye,' said Sal, dragging ghoulishly at the skin beneath her eyeball to give them a good look at the red-veined material she is made of.

Afterwards I congratulated Sal and asked her where her newfound boldness had come from.

'I've been keeping a diary,' she said. 'I write down everything, especially things said by nasty girls. And inside the front cover I've written: *This diary must be published as soon as possible*.'

Beth went out this evening, with Axel. Is it to talk about the house, I asked.

'I hope not,' said Beth.

She was wearing a dress with a short skirt, and her face looked different – it was the mascara, I decided. I was going to say something typically fraternal about the neckline and the hem, but then thought better of it. You look wonderful, I said. Have a great time. Beth, my sister who probably knows how to hang a door, blushed.

'What'll you do about supper for Sal?' she asked.

Maybe we'll walk down to Kalky's for fish and chips, I said.

Which we did. It was a warm, windless evening and Kalk Bay was awake as if it were daytime. A convivial row of fishermen on the pier cast out their lines. Sons and daughters helped to attach wriggling bits of bait to hooks; wives unpacked large bottles of fizzy cooldrink. Many of the boats are named after wives or womenfolk, I notice: Mary Jane, and my favourite, Marion Dawn. If I had a boat, I could call it Theresa.

We like Kalky's because it has absolutely no pretensions. Whether you order crayfish or hake it is slapped on your picnic table in the same styrofoam container. The tomato sauce is served in a sawn-off plastic juice bottle.

I recognised one of the women deep-frying fish as a girl I'd been to catechism with as a child. Rochelle Fernandez, the name came back to me. The boy John loved her thick straight black hair, probably handed down through generations of Kalk Bay families, starting with the first Filipino forebear who jumped ship at Simon's Town. I remembered how once, on our walk back from St James to Kalk Bay after one of Father Nolan's classes, I picked up the discarded ring of a beer can in the gutter and, handing it to her, asked her to marry me. I wondered if she was entertaining the same recollection.

'Haven't seen you in church recently, John,' she observed. 'Do you want vinegar with that?'

We have come a long way since our moment of intensity, Rochelle Fernandez and I.

Sal and I played rummy till her eyelids drooped. She's asleep at last; Beth not yet home. I've got all the windows open to catch even the slightest breeze. It's high tide, and the waves are roaring.

This morning Sal, Beth and I took Mrs Cloete down
to the Haven night shelter's open day. First there was
a moment of consternation in which I thought my car
had been stolen, but then I remembered abandoning it
near Hillrise steps. Sal and I walked up to fetch it. We
collected Beth and Mrs Cloete and parked near the bottle
store so that she didn't have far to walk.

Outside the little tin railway shanty where it all happens,
a Kaapse band played their ramkietjies in a happy
monotone. Mrs Cloete was taken with the foot-tapping
music. Tiny the bergie was dancing with abandonment,
his jeans low on his hips. Mrs Cloete thought it looked
fun, so she shifted a few steps, cakewalked a moment in
a mirror image of him. Tiny rushed up, clasped her to
his bosom and swirled her about. Concerned that Mrs
Cloete might take a tumble, Beth intervened to release
her, much to the disappointment of the fish cleaners, and
the German tourist who was recording it all on video.

The shelter was selling things made by the homeless
– aprons, bags, and some rather Cezanne-like paintings.
I did all my Christmas shopping there (apart from Sal's
present, which has to be a toy) because I can't bear
shopping malls.

We bought bread and hummus from the Olympia
for lunch. We adults had a beer shandy while Sal mixed
herself a potent-looking chocolate milk drink.

I spent the rest of the day lying on my bed reading
a brilliant book called *The Heather Blazing* by Colm
Tóibín from cover to cover. The novel holds up a lantern
inside the mind of that particular kind of silent, reserved

and apparently unresponsive male I've never liked, so that I felt, as I read, that I was breaking through into an uncommon empathy.

For supper, Beth made a chilled avocado and cucumber soup. Sal helped me make a huge fruit salad for dessert with every possible thing in it: lychees, granadillas, paw-paw, strawberries, peaches. We ate it with a very fine vanilla ice cream.

Because I was missing you, I came in here this evening to reread some of your mails. The way I've saved them, I have to read my own, often passionate, words before I come to your measured replies. I didn't read the ones from the beginning of our affair, that would be too painful. But these recent letters of yours, free from ardour, are just as poignant. There is so much that you leave out, both in your communication with Theo and with me. So much of your life is subterranean, like the two-thirds of Ayer's Rock that no one sees. From your steady replies, your interested questions and comments, I can see that you want this correspondence to continue. But either you never think of me with desire, or you are engaged in a frightening project of self-censorship. Or do women really think of sex less often than men?

If you were to die, and Theo to find only the mails of this year (mine somehow expunged), he would find very little to incriminate you. Except for the fact that you write to me at all.

Sunday 22nd December
11.59 pm

This morning I thrashed through my early cold swim

192

with the anger that is a thin disguise for despair, or its harbinger. Having forgotten my towel, I dried myself on my shirt and then walked bare-chested home in the chill air. The streets have become a series of molehills and ditches surrounded by red and white striped tape as Telkom and the electricity department lay new pipes under the old cobbled roads. I would like to go down there, into the underground of the village, find a penny or a farthing from long ago, or 1920s worker graffiti, or yesterday itself, or our trapped messages.

I came home to find a funeral in progress. Though it looked like sleep, Mrs Gray's head was tucked permanently under her wing. In the mist that often precedes a hellishly hot day, with the surviving doves cooing from trees and power lines above, Sal and Beth, still in their pyjamas, lowered Mrs Gray in her All-Bran coffin into a grave below the baboon statue in the garden. The Anglican church bell tolled.

Axel came to tea. So did Vera and Ryno. Beth had made a fruit cake and Ryno brought some wicked chocolate things from his local deli at the Noordhoek farm village. For our entertainment, Sal acted out Mrs Cloete's visit to the night shelter's open day. Young Alan obliged by taking the role of Tiny.

Tea turned into drinks. Axel and Beth were talking about the rare antique hinge he needs to get to repair the dresser, and the possibility of searching shops with names like Baltic Timbers and Wynberg Handlebar. Meanwhile, I was telling Vera about how I am on kissing terms now with Tizzy Clack, my old enemy. It was a private conversation but when I said 'kissing terms' everyone stopped their conversations and in amazing unison turned to me (Beth and Ryno's voices booming loudest): 'On kissing terms with who?' Except that Mrs

Cloete said: 'Ron kissing Germans too?'

Later Vera and I took the children to Fish Hoek beach for a night swim. There is a floodlight at the corner, so one is not in the pitch dark. The waves were perfect for bodysurfing, breaking on our moving bodies and forcing us forward with their impetus. Then a black, slippery shape brushed past Vera in the water. She shrieked and clung to me; Sal and Alan soon appended themselves too. When the seal popped up again, showing its friendly, doggy snout, we laughed with relief.

Vera and Alan had walked to our house earlier in the day, so I drove them home after dropping Sal with Beth. Vera and I sat talking till late, Alan asleep on the sofa next to us, and not much red wine left in the bottle.

Tuesday 24th December
5.15 pm

I am writing this on a cool, rainy Christmas Eve. It always gets cool just before Christmas.

I've skipped a day – I must catch up. Yesterday blasted out an inferno heat and hellish wind. I started it with a good icy swim. Even though I pulled on my swimming trunks the moment I woke up at 6.30 am, there were already people in Dalebrook pool. There is a woman who swims in goggles and snorkel: she never lifts her head. This means that she feels perfectly entitled to swim back and forth without swerving to avoid oncoming swimmers. I promise that I only thought briefly of stopping up her air spout with my thumb. There is another woman who finds the water too cold to enter completely, so she stands half-immersed, holding the rail and preventing others from making a safe descent. And dogs, everyone seems to bring their dogs. Some sniff your towel and possessions, making you look fearfully back from the pool in case your clothes are about to be urinated upon; others are anxious about their owners and bark at them to come out, or run perilously up and down the slippery tidal wall, tracking them. Others simply dive in and doggy-paddle along.

In October and even November, I can swim alone. Seven in the morning is too early or not warm enough for the crowds. In October, you can still see whales breaching, and hear them blowing. Always on calm days there are kayaks gliding, and in almost all weathers, a fishing boat near the horizon. I rest my arms on the wet wall, look across at Simon's Town bay in the distance and the harbour with its protective dolosse in the foreground, and say to myself, This is your life. It is hard to believe I am so lucky. If you were me, you'd resist this self-satisfied complacency. You would be worried about the fishermen's quotas, you'd want to organise swimming lessons for the children of Congolese refugees, you'd volunteer at the night shelter.

Everyone's here now – the seasonal visitors, the day trippers, bus tours, family from overseas. I am still lucky, because while they are stuck in bumper-to-bumper traffic, I saunter past with my towel around my neck. But I don't like the crowds, feel a terrible sense of ennui and déjà vu about how, despite the pink evenings, the champagne, the parties and the warm sea, the abiding impression will be of the crush of humanity, leaving behind their chicken bones and cigarette butts and plastic packets and broken glass. Somebody's drunken father will rise up from the tidal pool with a wig of seaweed on his head, and this will cause more hilarity, and more aunties will be tempted to wade in wearing their clothes, there will be calls for more wine and in the morning, children will have to sidestep used condoms in the car park.

Everyone is talking about their Christmas arrangements. As I was entering the subway after my swim, I heard a man say, 'We'll be twenty-four at dinner tonight. I'll have to do a second turkey on the Weber.'

Well, we won't 'be twenty-four', and I draw the line at turkey, but we are having a party. Ryno is coming to braai a fish – yellowtail probably – and Mrs Cloete is going to make coleslaw 'with all the trimmings' – I think she means a sour cream and cumin seed dressing. Hannelie is coming with Harriet. She's making a chocolate mousse. Sal asked what there'd be for *her* to eat. Beth said she'd make potato wedges in garlic for her. 'And no little sticks,' said Sal. The 'little sticks' are bits of chopped rosemary. Oh, and Axel the builder is coming.

I still can't quite absorb the fact of Sal eating again. The not-eating Sal will stay a while, I think, a ghostly shadow. But yesterday real Sal stood in the garden eating a huge chocolate-covered ice cream on a stick. 'Look, John,' she said, 'I'm normal.' If I cast my mind back, I'd be tempted to say that it was the point at which she started to get sassy, answer back, that marked her recovery.

Yesterday I saw Claire the psychologist in the Olympia café. I was leaving, and she and Angie were standing near the door waiting for a table. I nearly walked straight into them. I've never felt such a complex emotion. Right near the surface is dislike, the aversion we feel to people who have misunderstood us, or perhaps, more honestly, who have refused to buy into our myth. My deeper response is one of what I can only term resentful gratitude. She made a timely intervention. She stopped the anorexia monster in its tracks. Which is just what one would expect from Miss Clavell: perpetual vigilance.

I muttered a greeting as I passed her. John the recalcitrant schoolboy again.

This morning I woke up at five and decided to skip the crowds and go straight to the beach for a walk. As I passed Sal's room, I saw her sitting up eagerly in bed, opening a window of the advent calendar. Sal is really keen on Christmas, looking forward to her presents, I'm afraid. I whispered to her did she want to come along to the beach. She quickly pulled on a pair of elasticated trousers. We both looked down and saw that her supposedly long cotton pants now reached way above her ankles.

You've grown a hem's worth, Sal, I said.

The beach was strewn with a tide line of bluebottles. Sal hopped from one to the next, snapping them with the impact of her sandals. Sal snaps the bluebottle tap.

I am so used to walking alone that it was strange to have Sal's incessant conversation. She says she wants to be a bird tamer (she spent last Friday happily playing with Harriet's budgies) and a writer, perhaps combining the two and taking the budgie around for book signings. She asked so many questions about the animal kingdom (Can you ride carthorses? Do hermit crabs care about their babies? How do owls rotate their heads? Is a shark a fish? Why can a donkey suckle a zebra but not a horse?) that I wonder if this is an indication of a career direction.

Wednesday 25th December
5.59 pm

Happy Christmas, Theresa.

Our braai last night was such a success that we

have planned another for Friday evening. Beth printed Christmas carols from the internet and we sang them lustily till our neighbour stuck his head out and asked for a Silent Night.

This morning while Beth and Sal were at mass, I climbed up the ladder to the attic to look for the Father Christmas outfit my father used to wear. It wasn't a real, commercially made suit, but consisted of my father's scarlet PhD gown, a piece of ermine, a false beard and a white judge's wig – all these props from a theatrical costumier and donated by Mrs Cloete. I think Hugo had worn the stuff in a play once and not returned it.

It was hot and airless, and difficult to find anything in the mess. I buggered around with the torch and swore a bit, but the mission was successful. While I was up there, I saw a cardboard box that I recognised from long ago. It contained all my father's unpublished manuscripts, typed and filed in old, slightly textured ring binders.

All my childhood, I remember my father typing away in his study. My mother and Beth brought him his meals on a tray, often with a tiny vase of flowers or a saved piece of chocolate for his pudding. He sent his stories off, but they were hardly ever accepted for publication. Just before he died – I was about fifteen, and getting very high marks for English at school – he asked me what I planned to study, to be. I said, to study English, of course, to *be* a writer.

He nodded his head. It made sense for me to go to university. I could get a reduction of fees on two counts, both of them being academics. Neither of my parents would dream of pressing me to get a 'real' job.

What did I expect from my BA, asked my father.

Well, I said, I notice that all the writers I admire quote a great deal; they know all the ancient myths and have read the French poets in the original. I would like to be like them. I would like to be learned.

'Ah,' said my father, and gave me a very affectionate smile. 'Perhaps in that case you'll be tempted to study further, for a Master's degree, or even a doctorate?'

I said that I supposed so, if it turned out I was good enough.

'Oh, you'll be good enough, all right,' he said, 'no problem there. But if you keep studying, you might become a scholar, not a writer.'

Can't the two go together, I asked.

'Look at me,' said my father. 'Look at all these paltry short stories, these unpublished fragments of mine. That's all I've managed to produce, in between departmental meetings, research, teaching. It takes it out of you. All your energies go elsewhere. And your whole career is premised on an attitude of awe towards other writers. You never see yourself as their peer. You genuflect before their greatness. You write small, small, mousey stories, as if you think it would be an impertinence to go for the grand flourish, to open your lungs and give of your full range. You know that I've never been a great one for giving advice, boy, but I hope you'll consider this: don't go further than an Honours degree. Oh, read all you like, do whatever private study takes your fancy. But remember: a writer writes.'

My father did try to write, in between crisis meetings in the English department and managing a huge teaching load. And research. He was working on a project to do with John Keats's letters, in collaboration with another Romantic scholar in Pretoria. Then John Keats briefly entered world news: the poet's last remaining letter had been discovered, where, but in Pretoria. And not by my father or his scholarly colleague. They were crushed, humiliated. I'm sure that's what weakened his heart. Or perhaps it is a genetic condition, God forbid. He also loved butter. To die at fifty-five seems terribly young.

I inherited his little portable typewriter – actually, it was state of the art at the time. I typed away like archy, but I was aiming for the prose style of Somerset Maugham. He was probably the one writer on my father's shelf whose stories I could read with ease at thirteen or fourteen. Though I read my way solidly through all the Penguin classics, whether I understood them or not.

Poetry was even trickier. Sometimes a poem would mean nothing, nothing at all, till you'd read or were given an explication. Still, I wanted to be admitted to the secret society of those who read and unravelled and wrote verse. TS Eliot was my first introduction to Modernism, and I was so fascinated by his 'rhythmical grumbling' that my father took me up to campus one day when I was still a schoolboy to hear a Summer School Lecture on *The Waste Land*. I sat there gobsmacked, not understanding a single word of advanced literary scholarship, but still drawn to its mysteries. On the exam pad I'd brought along to take notes I wrote my name, over and over: JS Carson. It looked good. Initials are important for poets.

At school, in Standard Five, we wrote poems. One topic was 'Rain'. I sat there stunned, wondering what, what, to say about rain? I looked over Ryno's shoulder. He had written: 'Splash! Plop!/ A falling drop'. I remember thinking that was damn good, envying him. I waited for an inner voice. Nothing came. Ryno was still writing furiously. Seemingly he had no end of onomatopoeia to pour onto the page. He had cracked this poetry thing, he had it waxed. All you did was describe the thing in the way it had always been described, and in rhyme.

We only had a few minutes left. My page was still

blank. Then it came through. It came from nowhere.
There was the blank page, then there were words:

Rain
Across the veld sweeps the sky's great grey grief.
Poised on hardened earth, buck scent their relief.
I open my mouth, feel drops on my tongue.
It beats on hot tin; I do not miss the sun.
Bring rain, sing rain, sources still unseen:
it feeds us all; it washes sinners clean.

I was still a good Catholic boy in those days, you understand.

I remember my teacher picking up my page and
reading. I was trembling, there was a crisis inside me. She
had to like it, she just had to, I was completely done for
if she didn't. Miss Black was a big woman with somewhat
pronounced fangs and a sarcastic turn of phrase. But I
trusted her judgement; I knew she had that elusive thing
we call taste.

At last she looked up and said, 'I'm keeping this for
the school magazine, John. You really have the most
extraordinary way with words.'

I nearly burst with pride and happiness. I wonder if
teachers know how their comments stay with us, how just
one compliment, genuinely meant, can change the course
of a life?

I wrote poems at home, too, but it felt shameful to be
writing without a charge or commission. I sent them to
a strange nuts-and-yoga type magazine called Odyssey,
but asked the editor if he published them to print them
anonymously or under a pseudonym. The editor knew
my parents, phoned them and said I'd written some
good poems and that I mustn't be silly about my name. I

should feel proud. Of course this was the first my parents had heard about me and poetry. They put on their glasses and read the poems. They didn't say much. I assumed they didn't like them and I felt crushed.

In my juvenilia there is a lot about the veld and nature. I thought that's what one wrote about. Like Paton: *There is a lovely road that runs from Ixopo into the hills.* Later I thought the topic ought to be oppression, violence, atrocity. Like Serote: *if i pour paraffin on a white child's face.* At last, I turned inwards, described what I saw. But my voice was dull and flat until I started to write with you in mind. I am no dancer, but with you I am light on my feet:

I like to lean in you; I live to urge
and lure you. Watch my feet, now watch my eyes.
Stop all others. This is how we do it.
I take your waist, you hold my shoulder. Lift.
Listen to the tune. Trust my every move.
You have come for me; I have come for you.

I came down from the attic and dressed up as Father Christmas, though I couldn't see how to attach the beard. I put all the presents in a hessian sack. Still the others weren't back. I waited in the sitting room, staring blankly at the nativity scene we'd made in August out of clay and dog hair, and more recently pepped up with craft paint. I prayed: Dear God, this is John. I miss you and the swinging incense and the feeling of holiness on Christmas days in my childhood. Help me to be a better person.

Then Mrs Cloete came in and helped me to be a bearded person with spirit gum. Ryno arrived and took his mother out to lunch.

After opening the presents, we ate last night's leftovers.

I set out the food and washed up. I knew I should offer to entertain Sal, but I didn't have the stamina. She was happy with the three trolls she'd got from me. I just had to lie down on my bed and have a nap. Later I heard Ron arrive. When I popped my head into her room, the two of them were playing a very good game, 'You are the weakest troll'. I thought, trust Ron to bring everything back to TV. But they seemed happy.

I would like to have a nap with you one day, but I don't know how much actual rest we'd get.

Thursday 26th December
4.45 pm

There is a dog in Kalk Bay who bays along with emergency sirens. He howls long and sad when ambulances, fire trucks or police cars go shrieking by in the Main Road. I wonder what melancholy association he makes in his doggy mind, what canine tragedy lurks there. It seems that people get into lots of scrapes on Boxing Day because the sirens, and the dog's mournful echo, ring out throughout the day.

Christmastime depresses me. I think it is because of the compulsory socialising. I like to hear the news from my family and friends in the ordinary haphazard, spontaneous course of events. I like to capture people in flight, as they flit to their next task or appointment, uttering a running commentary as they go. But to have to sit down opposite Sal, Beth, Ryno, Mrs Cloete and the rest with a mince pie in my paw and actually make leisurely conversation, not to be allowed to come here and write because we are all 'having a good time' like in Fugard's play, that is too tedious for words.

I always miss you, but more at Christmas. My mother, too, I miss her. I want to die like her. Not in the same way as her, but with the same uncomplaining fortitude. After the first stroke, she was indignant at the impairment of her speech, and the slight paralysis of her body. Though it hadn't affected her mind, she had to stop teaching briefly because of the slurred speech. When she returned to campus, articulate again, she sensed the change in power relations immediately. In the kindest way, the university made it clear they didn't need her any more, put her under pressure to retire even though students still clamoured to be admitted to her seminars or be supervised by her. She said it was knowing that there were plenty of good younger women to take her place that made her accept, reluctantly, that it was time to step down.

Of course she did all the prescribed therapy, the stretching and the pulleys. Her best graduate students still visited her, brought her their papers to crit. And then Mrs Cloete said she'd like to be introduced to feminist theory, which gratified my mother and I think really interested her too – it was a major project. Ma was gallant, accepted the new limitations – not driving, not Head of the Gender Institute, not in charge, but still esteemed.

Then, just when she'd recuperated, the second stroke came. Again she endured physio and speech therapy, but with less commitment than before. This distinguished woman who had always been animated, fully present, lapsed into listlessness. It was October 2000. I came down from your farm one weekend to look after her. She said she'd like a swim. I thought it would be all right, she'd been doing her exercises, and swimming is always therapeutic. We went to the corner at Fish Hoek, put our towels beneath the clock. She was seventy years old, but her figure was still girlish, though perhaps a little on the thin side, and you could still see that one side of the body was carrying the other. There was a light, crisp breeze and the waves were coming in clean sets. I stayed with her till she seemed to be swimming at her ease. Then I struck out as usual, aiming for the round house at Sunny Cove as my marker. I turned back at one point to check on her, but she wasn't there. I was puzzled, peering. Something was wrong. I swam back inshore as rapidly as I could. Two men – a father and son, I think – were lifting my mother's frail, limp body out of the water. She'd decided to cut her swim short, she'd been returning to the shore, when a wave had come from behind and felled her.

We helped her to her feet. She spluttered and staggered. Her mouth hung open and her skin was an unhealthy yellow. The shoulder strap of her costume slipped off and she was briefly exposed. I wrapped her towelling gown around her. The men helped me get her to the car. They were terribly solicitous. My mother didn't speak, only nodded her head that she was all right.

She hardly spoke again after that, though she lived another two weeks. Our GP came and checked her out; said, 'I hear you've been buffeted,' and pronounced her 'basically fit'. But something had happened to her that was not physical. She had always been completely independent and something more than that – dignified. Now she had been humiliated, I think. She ate very little after that – nothing really – just weak tea or grape juice brought up by tiny Sal on a wobbling tray. One morning Beth found she'd died in her sleep, her hands composed upon her chest as if to say: I intended this.

It is the loneliness that strikes one.

Your gifts arrived: thank you. A first edition of *archy
and mehitabel* – I can just imagine the lengths you went
to to get that. And a new white cotton shirt, collarless.
With a message attached in your precious handwriting
– 'What poets need'. No more jokes about John Carson's
checked shirts. I feel especially privileged because I know
you must have smuggled these things to your holiday
house and covertly arranged their transport to me. If
the courier company phones about suing you or me, it's
because of the story I'm about to relate.

Ryno was here with Sir Nicholas for lunch. Luckily, I
still had a can of dog food left in the cupboard. We were
sitting out the back with our beers in hand and thick slices
of bread and snoek pâté. Quite suddenly Sir Nicholas
looked up from his trough, detecting an intruder at the
front door. The courier had probably been ringing the
bell that says 'bell', except that it hasn't been connected
to a ring tone since 1951. Enraged, the dog charged and
barked. At this, the courier, a sturdy-looking young
woman, apparently vaulted over the spiked wooden fence
into the neighbour's property. I say 'apparently' because
when I arrived at the front door, I saw nothing out of the
ordinary. Beth handed me a clipboard with a consignment
note and said, 'You're going to get us sued one day.' She
had calmed Ryno's dog, and for a moment I didn't know
what she was talking about. But then I looked out. On the
other side of the fence there was a woman wearing only her
shirt and black tanga briefs, tatters of khaki around her
ankles, half giggling, half hysterical. I stared and stared at
this apparition. Every now and then the woman shouted

something at her driver, down at the gate. 'My pant, my whole pant is gone!' Pants, I said, your pants are gone.

I understood that your parcel had been delivered, but couldn't work out why the courier had no trousers on and why she kept trying to gather up the vestiges of them around her crotch. The more she stared down there, the more I did too. Then she vaulted over to our side, flapping strips of material, black briefs and all. 'I'll find you some pants,' I said at last, as I pieced together what had happened (but not the pants). Dazedly, I wandered around the house looking for something to give her, trying to think what size she was. Then I remembered some elasticated white beach pants of Beth's: she'd put them in the laundry cupboard and told me to give them to the next beggar. I showed the courier into the downstairs bathroom and handed her the pants. She was good-natured, almost hearty. Lucky the fence only caught her clothing, not her flesh.

Clothes are obviously today's theme. With great fanfare and much laughter, Tizzy Clack came to take Mrs Cloete shopping for an outfit to wear to Sunday's launch.

I also had to go shopping, for tonight's braai and Sunday's launch. I filled a huge trolley and bought lots of things we probably won't eat or don't need, just because the shop was so crowded and buzzing and I was a bit demented. The total rang up to R1 000. I felt quite sick at so much money. But I can claim back some of it from the trust. How I long for the quiet, party-free days of July.

The recycling has reached all-time toppling-over proportions. Tiny came earlier but only to exchange gifts. He doesn't really want to do my recycling, I realise. He gave me a dead pot plant and I gave him R20 and we wished each other compliments of the season. I've been doing a lot of housework lately. The bright summer sun has thrown our squalor into relief. Thus I was trying to polish the floor of the front room when Tiny rolled up, reeking of cheap wine but looking very lordly with a flower in his buttonhole.

When you're down on your knees, you see how intractable a problem dirt really is. Little things, remnants of past days, get wedged between the floorboards. I rubbed away and got a large splinter in my hand for my troubles. Sal pulled it out while I whimpered. Washing up is endless at this time of the year. I want to tell our visitors to bring their own crockery and cutlery and take it home to their own sinks afterwards.

Last night I went for a swim after eight. The sun had gone down, but many people were still on the beach. Everyone else was content to play in the breakers, but I wanted a good stretch, so I swam out as I usually do. The warm dark water lapped me like velvet. Though I still heard voices, the night saved me from the nearness of other bodies. 'Aren't you afraid of sharks?' someone called to me from the catwalk. The answer to that is no. I am afraid of whales, not sharks. A whale might accidentally come up for air beneath me. I love swimming. Apart from walking, it is the one sport I can do with ease.

As a fat (well, plump) little boy, I enjoyed the weightlessness of swimming. I did lengths in the Brass Bell pool, but never bothered to try out for teams at school. Until the school gala in 1979, nobody knew I could swim. A boy in the freestyle relay team, from my house, was ill, and at the last minute I was called upon to participate. Our team was trailing behind. I came powering through the water in my lap, but only managed to bring us into second place. Although I was congratulated, I was not satisfied. I realised that even though I'd never competed before, even though the situation was hopeless, I had wanted to win.

Must get things ready for the braai.

The day before has dawned quite calm and blue as if to say, 'what's wrong?' and perhaps nothing is, if the journal will just arrive today from Red's damn printer and if I can get rid of this hangover and if Hannelie and Ryno are still speaking to me after last night's disaster.

After the braai, the girls danced about the dark garden with sparklers, in and out of the hibiscus bushes. Hannelie joined them and swirled her bright pink skirts about. When she climbed girlishly into the tree and her dress got caught up in the branches, I saw both Red and Ryno taking a good peek.

The mood was good, but there was aggression in the air. Does that make sense? I think what I mean is that there was an undercurrent of male sniping. Things could have gone either way.

It started with Ryno asking Red whether his 'two-bit' printer buddy was going to get *The Unofficial View* out in time, and wouldn't it have been better to get in a professional? Red returned the favour by asking Ryno where he was hiring his 'tannoy system' from and telling him, 'We don't want any of your karaoke kak, hey, this is a high-class event'.

I thought maybe it was all quite light hearted. We'd

209

had a lot to drink, of course, not just wine with the meal and beer earlier. Ryno was deep into his second or third brandy and Coke and Red was tossing back some quite short gin and tonics. I had a whisky at hand but wasn't drinking in a dedicated way like the other two because I was putting pine-cones on the fire and fetching a rug for Mrs Cloete (the evening was growing chilly) and calling to the girls did they want ice cream.

Then Ryno thought he'd include me in his attempts at being humorous. 'I'm just teasing you,' he kept saying, but I was quite irritated. The drift of his 'teasing' was that it was a very good ruse on my part to go around posing as a poet, because 'chicks love that'. He also had a lot to say about my looks. 'It's that curly brown hair,' he mocked, 'and those eyelashes, such a pretty boy. A pretty poet. You wouldn't say he was pushing forty. He's pushing forty, y'know, Hannelie.' Hannelie called back jokingly that she was also pushing forty and it was like being a dung beetle.

I told him to come off it, but he kept goading me, in very poor taste. 'Remember that time you came out on a pass and screwed – sorry – scored all those friends of Beth's? You weren't even a poet's backside then. All you'd published was a couple of sonnets in the school magazine. Come on, Beth, back me up here. D'you remember?'

Hannelie and the girls had stopped playing: everyone was looking at me. Beth told Ryno to leave me alone, but he was having too much of a good time. He went up to Hannelie and did a mock come-on routine, backing her up against the garden wall and caging her by putting one arm against it. 'I reckon I must try it some time. Hey, Hannelie, I'm a poet. I write poetry.' He made the word sound prissy and affected. Hannelie giggled.

I don't know what got into me – I'd like to say it was the drink – but I went up to him so swiftly he couldn't prepare himself and locked my arm around his neck. We went struggling across the dark grass and we deadlocked, straining, far away from the fire, almost at the boundary wall of our property. The thick, damp smell of dew on torn-up lawn brought me to my senses. In low tones I suggested that a good idea would be to rise from the ground with easy dignity and rejoin the others at the fireside. We released by mutual easing of grips and sat again in friendly companionship side by side on a log with Red. I saw Sal go up to her mother and hold on tight.

Unfortunately, Red said: 'Poets: one; Photographers: nil.' Next thing I knew, it was Red and Ryno who were rolling down the slope in a deadlock. It didn't last long. I think Ryno quickly remembered Red's age, or noticed him drawing breath with difficulty, and so released him.

Mrs Cloete apologised for Ryno's behaviour. 'Hugo was just like that, I'm afraid, until he went queer.' This made Red guffaw and say, 'Well, Ryno, there's hope for you yet.'

Mrs Cloete said it was way past her bedtime. Beth cast us a scornful look. She and Axel helped the old lady back to her cottage. Hannelie and the girls started taking all the stuff inside. Axel came and said goodnight, he'd be going.

We men carried on sitting there, drinking in the dark. Every now and then Ryno would wrap his near arm around my neck and give it a tight squeeze. He kept up his teasing about poets, and about my hair. 'People expect more of you when you have naturally curly hair,' he said, 'that's a fact.'

And suddenly I blew. I SWORE at him. Fuck you! I yelled: YOU JUST DON'T STOP! I pushed him, I think, and then when we were both standing, with me repeating my two furious lines, I hit him with the blades of both hands on the chest and knocked him down. He just lay there. Jeez, he must've been drunk. Under normal circumstances there's no way I could have decked Ryno Cloete.

Beth, Frances and Hannelie came running. 'This is quite enough!' shouted Beth. 'You're all drunk. I'm completely disgusted at all of you.' Red took this opportunity to fall drunkenly off the back of the log. Frances went to help her husband, who was now reciting Tennyson's Ulysses. Hannelie bent over Ryno to check his vital signs. He reached up and grabbed her, pulling her down onto the ground. 'I love you, baby,' he said. I was about to help Hannelie when I saw the affectionate look she was giving Ryno.

'So that's what it was all about,' I said.

Sunday 29th December
2.30 pm

Three hours to go to the launch. I am so nervous I am ready to pass out. The part of me that copes with public speaking and crowded occasions has arrived; I can already see my real self smiling a little apologetically at me from the doorway as he departs.

After what happened on Friday, I've no idea whether Ryno will pitch up this evening to set up the stage and the mike, though I feel sure Hannelie won't let me down with the wine.

But the copies arrived! They were here all the time, in fact. At lunch time yesterday I was in a state close to panic. *The Unofficial View* hadn't arrived, Red hadn't phoned, and I confess I felt too nervous to phone him. I didn't want him to think I don't trust him or his little man in Claremont. I knew I was part of the reason the little man was having to do a rush job.

I sat drinking tea with Beth and discussing emergency plans. Then Sal walked in and said, 'What's wrong?' I told her how anxious I was about the non-arrival of the journal and she looked stupefied: 'But there's a note on the front table from Mrs Cloete saying that Red's wife dropped a few copies off with her while you were swimming and that everything is on track.'

It looks good: Red's printer has done well.

I've spent the day making snacks. The menu is fillet on French bread, peppered mackerel on Duen's wholewheat, crudités and dips, snoek pâté, leek pies, mini drop scones with sour cream and a sprinkle of caviar, pizza-breads from Hennie's Market, cheese and biscuits. I went way over budget.

Vera has been helping me. She's gone home now to shower and change, promises to arrive looking like a flamenco dancer.

Monday 30th December
4.45 pm

This morning I swam out to the buoy. Beyond the breakers, the water was utterly clear. Far down beneath me I could see the wrinkled sand of the ocean floor. The sensation of weightlessness matched my inner feeling of relief. Relief, but also a strange bubble of emptiness, my temporary preoccupations departed.

I forgot to feed the fish, but it succeeded in attracting my attention by dragging its belly against the gravel noisily as I walked past Sal's room after my shower. She, of course, wouldn't dream of feeding it, has completely lost interest in its fate. You are a very clever fish, I said, as I sprinkled its flakes.

The launch is over. It was, as far as I can judge, a success. Two people have phoned saying they have never enjoyed poetry so much.

When Beth, Sal, Mrs Cloete and I arrived at the hall with the snacks, Ryno and Hannelie were already there. Ryno came straight up to me and shook my hand, apologising for Friday night. I said no, no, I should never have allowed our altercation to become physical. There were tears in his eyes. What a pair they'll make. Hannelie, who had set out the glasses, now entered with great armfuls of flowers of the same deep crimson colour as her sari-like dress. She moved quickly about the hall, arranging flowers, finding chairs, her hair flaming out behind her and her wrap skirt opening to reveal the occasional flash of attractive thigh. Ryno's eyes followed her from his sound desk: he was rewarded with a glowing smile.

I was doing a sound test for Ryno when Red and Frances arrived. There was more shaking of hands. Red made a point of admiring the sound system; Ryno seemed to think *The Unofficial View* looked stunning.

The room filled with people. One minute Sal and Harriet were dancing across an empty wooden floor, the next it was standing room only. The Arts editor of the morning daily came up and introduced herself.

'You even look like a poet,' she said.

It's the shirt, I replied.

'I think this is a wonderful occasion,' she said. 'I'm

going to write it up. Poetry ... Kalk Bay: the two seem to go together. And isn't that Audrey Cloete, the actress?'

I followed her eyes to where Mrs Cloete sat, surrounded by poets who had at last found a genuine reader. Tizzy Clack had helped her select a splendid outfit: a beautiful long cotton shirt in the deepest green, with dark green jeans and long necklaces strung with multi-shaped beads. Her white hair looked as though it had been professionally blow-dried. Her beauty had come back. I tried to catch her eye, but she was too deeply involved in conversation.

Red gave a warm, off-the-cuff introduction. Then it was my turn to speak. I thanked the Feinstein Trust and gave a little background about the genesis of the edition. Nothing that I said was true. I mean, I didn't mention the coloured pencils, or Mrs Cloete's role, or the dagga, or the child's game that brought out Vusi's poem, or my satirical request that set Vera off. I thanked Red, Hannelie and Ryno but obviously didn't describe how we'd all got fall-down drunk and abused one another in a late-night orgy in front of minors. I talked vaguely about 'serendipity' and 'good fortune'. The Feinstein trustees smiled benignly.

Then I read something I'd prepared. I introduced my speech by saying that I was sure many people in the room found poets and poetry intriguing. Perhaps they struggled to understand poetry. Perhaps they struggled to write it. I went on:

Let me imagine that you have asked me how one writes a poem. There is of course no recipe for a poem. You might say that poetry is an offshoot of the poet's personality. Poems emerge out of the excess of that personality. If the poet drinks too much, takes too many drugs, commits suicide, steals husbands

215

or wives, hears the voices of the dead, burns poems, resorts to incest, walks too far, dies too young, defiles the body's temple, spirals into madness, that is not in itself the mark that sets the poet apart, but the excess of excess.

The poet is a lonely person, feels always that the team has been picked already and that he has been left out. Perforce, he becomes an eavesdropper, a spy. He rejoices at his solitude. He loathes his solitude. Pariah, he calls himself, loathsome outcast. He scorns the group. He longs for the group's approbation. Oh, but I am wonderful, he sings, I am the very heartbeat of the world. He affects not to care, but he cares too much.

Poetry is an expression of this too-muchness. The poet puts down, expiates, an excess of feeling – all feeling. Even or especially rage, jealousy, indignation, grief, depression, hatred, but also empathy, compassion, sorrow, wryness, joy, lust, laughter, irony. The poet cannot contain these feelings or their contradictions. They wake him up at night with their drum roll and their drum beat, with their catchy sounds and their inner life, their lively, deathly insistent voices demanding notation, dictation. If the poet hesitates, says he is tired, he is hungry, or there is a living to be earned, then the voices redouble, become cleverer or more subtle. They use echoes and refrains, skip or repeat a certain beat, they drive, drive, drive the poet to his page. Don't ask me how a poem is written, ask me how a poem is *not* written.

The poet is shy, he does not speak aloud. Or, he wishes to speak aloud, but some crushing, bruising language mangler is dominating the floor. The poet is flayed by what he hears and prevented from escape by what is still left to say. He must take up the knife, if need be he must wrest it — the ripper's jackknife, the surgeon's scalpel, the wit's rapier, the fencer's épée, the fishwife's gutter, the pirate's dagger, the chef's cleaver, the craftsman's blade. He must make, and he must break.

If you cannot be a poet, do not walk away from poetry. Stay and console the poet. The silent poet is not really blank, merely unpublished. Ask him for a poem. Or one dark night, when her pupils are dilated with the fear of her own thoughts, *that one talent which is death to hide*, whisper in her ear: 'You *are* a poet.'

When I'd finished, I introduced Vusi, who read 'Give the poet what he needs'. Ryno had organised a backing track that sounded a bit like the Soweto String Quartet. Then the others read: Tizzy Clack, the Mountain Club, Girisha. Girisha's beauty was accentuated by the way she supported old Hector Newbury up to the podium. You could see he was quite smitten with her. (She was lambent, I realised with shock; truly she was radiant.) Barbara Daniels made them weep; Catherine Magwaza made them cheer. No one wanted to leave — the party just kept going. I went upstairs at one point, out onto the balcony with the smokers. The Christmas fairy lights are up in the village, everything twinkles.

I got home just after midnight, but I couldn't sleep. My head roared with noise. Conversations kept replaying themselves. I regretted my speech — it was too much of a rhetorical flourish, full of stupid generalisations, not light enough. But I felt proud of my friends and the poets, the audience too.

Now what? A sudden hollowness.

It is the end of the year and I'm consumed with a sense of loathing for everything and everyone. The problem with New Year is that there is nothing 'new' about it or the three hundred and sixty-five days it heralds. Tonight all the world's silly, unthinking louts and bimbos will party, and at the stroke of twelve let out loud, meaningless yelps from the belly of their pre-literate selves. Doubtless some drunken brawler will be pushed into the Brass Bell pool and I will hear the echo of his assailants' guffaws ricocheting off the mountain above me. I would like to go in there and break up their tables like Jesus.

I want someone to tell me: what is there to celebrate? I have another bleak year of separation from you to look forward to, sending you these long letters, receiving your dashed-off responses which you squeeze in, between buying wheelchairs and rehabilitating the poor. I will continue to eke out a living while you enjoy long holidays with your husband who did not cry for your son, but cried enough to keep you, and all the time my body will keep shrivelling to a discarded husk for want of your touch.

Even my friends and family irritate me. Couples, couples, couples: I am surrounded by them. Well, two at least: Hannelie twined around Ryno; Beth tentatively dating Axel. And don't forget the perennially happily married Red and Frances. Even Harriet and Sal are a twosome. They all wanted to have a New Year's Eve party here, the cynical Vera too, but I told them I've had it with parties and mindless social interaction. I heard them in the kitchen yesterday (yes, I was eavesdropping on the stairs) planning to have it at Hannelie's house in the Marina. Good for them, if they feel they have something to look forward to. I shall stay here and eat toast and drink no toasts and be pleased not to be making yet another plate of snacks.

Doubtless you will drink one tonight with Theo. Standing on some elegant Hermanus balcony at sunset, wearing a pretty dress and sparkling sandals, you will raise your glass to his, and later, when the New Year is counted in, you and your friends will kiss each other and shake hands. Someone will take a photograph of you all, with your prosperously raised glasses, grouped around a table with a large platter of fresh oysters as its centrepiece. It is nothing, or only a little thing, or shall I say just one more link in the chainsaw that keeps us apart.

Theresa, I can't keep going like this. I want to be released. Let me go.

You tell me it wasn't a decision, wasn't a choice, but your saying that doesn't stop me from perceiving it as one. You chose Theo. There was a crisis, a hiatus, a moment in your marriage when you could have changed everything, but you didn't. I don't want to be your platonic lover. I want to make you your favourite spinach and feta sauce while you sit at the kitchen table and talk with your hands. I want to listen to you and fill your glass. I want to hear all your plans for alleviating hunger, uplifting the squalid, comforting the desolate, buying wheels for the legless. I want to say something funny and watch you laugh. I want your eagerness and your ardour. I want you not always as a poet longs, but as a man wants.

You don't know how bad it is because I haven't told you. I write and write until it seems I have said everything, but still I leave things out. I have left out what happened with Vera.

At the end of August, that day when Vera was quizzing me in the Olympia café before Hannelie arrived, I didn't disclose our full conversation. It's true I was relieved when Hannelie interrupted us, but that was because Vera had just put the most extraordinary proposition to me and I was caught off guard.

'The difference between me and Hannelie,' said Vera, 'is that Hannelie wants to fall in love. I just want a lover. I'd like to be a scarlet woman. I love that sudden rush of hormones, the hunger of the first days. I'm not interested in looking after a man. Never stay with anyone long enough to find out what they look like when they're eating a mielie, is my philosophy. The thought of the long-term appals me. A brief liaison is what I have in mind. Someone to take upstairs with me at midnight, and who'll leave by dawn. What I'm saying, John, is come up and see me some time. Alan is spending the weekend with his father. I have a very good bottle of red wine I'd like an excuse to open.'

Aghast would be a good word to describe my response. But then I really thought about it. She is attractive, fun to be with. She is a poet. She is lonely. I have been told by you that you will in future be accompanied by Theo at every turn. Surely something very terrible will happen to me if I don't have sex soon?

Saturday, I said. I'll see you then. Could we make it before midnight?

'Sure,' she said, 'but I don't cook.'

I'll make something, I said.

'Well, as long as it's not mielies.'

Then Hannelie came in.

I went, of course. Still slightly fuzzy headed from the

night before's razzle at Ferdinand's restaurant. I made a risotto with homemade chicken stock, mushrooms and basil pesto. I'm sure you don't care, but I've always told you everything.

> *Last night, ah, yesternight, betwixt her lips and*
>   *mine*
> *There fell thy shadow, Cynara! thy breath was shed*
> *Upon my soul between the kisses and the wine;*
> *And I was desolate and sick of an old passion,*
> *Yea, I was desolate and bow'd my head:*
> *I have been faithful to thee Cynara! in my fashion.*

As an idealistic undergraduate, still vaguely believing in true love, I could not understand Ernest Dowson's poem, or why we had to study it. I probably even joined in the sniggering over his need to call for 'madder music and for stronger wine'. It seemed to me he was trying to have his cake and eat it. Why was he sleeping with a prostitute if he loved Cynara? But now that I know what it is to be 'desolate and sick of an old passion', I am less cynical.

I think it's a poem much quoted, a poem that has endured despite its mannered style, because it's got this strongly expressed paradoxical message about faithful faithlessness, which is self-justifying (and thus false, a pretence) but also so absolutely true of human nature. I suppose you could say it operates on two levels: the speaker is cheerfully self-deluding, the poet is mockingly observant. The key is Cynara, and how she feels about a lover who claims that though he has crushed someone else to his breast, she is still and forever first in his heart. But a poem like this forever excludes Cynara from answering back; she is the speaker's mythical creation of perfect love.

221

I'm not trying to avoid the issue by resorting to literary criticism. I just want to find a way of telling you the truth. Which is that when I walked through the dark village to Vera's house that night and on subsequent nights (though infrequently, since I was not in hot pursuit and we were driven by her whims and dependent on young Alan's infrequent visits to his father) I thought about you and I missed you.

Vera talks a lot about her writing, which makes me quite silent about mine. She does not reach out to humanity, as you do, but rather mocks it. But I like her. I like to listen to her. And she has helped with the bleakness. I will never be properly close to her, though. I think of all the things you know about me. I cannot imagine ever telling another woman those things. They are yours. I am yours.

But don't make me go through another year of this impuissance, of egg-timer visits, of helpless longing. I love your presents, but I cannot live without your presence. Come, Theresa, or summon me.

I'd like to say no. I'd like to be strong. Why should I fly to this assignation as if it weren't degrading? Because if someone knocks on the door while we're there, you know I'll have to hide or, worse, pretend to be an interior decorator. Measuring madam's new curtains for her grand holiday home. *I've always admired this house from the catwalk, always wondered what it looked like inside. You and your guests always look so fine on your veranda, sipping champagne, eating oysters. It's an honour to show you these very fine swatches. Have you seen these imported Warner fabrics with a summer feel?*

And which bed should we use, Theresa, when I come for my ration? Should we leave the master bedroom locked, Theresa, so that I don't have to contemplate Theo's choice of after-shave, or the counterpane of your Saturday nights?

And what shall I do when Theo phones, as he certainly will, to find out if you are fine, to enquire whether the curtain-measuring is coming along fine? What shall I do while you ask him tenderly: How is it on the farm? How is the young tree training going? And when you listen, smiling as if he were there in the room with us? What shall I do then, Theresa, how shall I comport myself? And when it's your turn to speak and you laugh and say into the mouthpiece, 'Oh, darling, you're not reading that old book again, are you? Goodness.' What should I do then, Theresa? I could look down at my feet, at the hairs on my toes, trying to remind myself that I'm real. Or I could slip discreetly off to another room. And when you return, I could look up and smile, as if I were truly delighted that Theo is well, as if my gut were not feeding off my very heart. I could even comment, lightly, Theo reading *The Good Soldier* again? How quaint he is.

Is this kind? Is this esprit de corps?

You say you feel a 'pang' when you read about Vera. But you would like me to pursue happiness wherever I find it. These are your words, your hermetically sealed words. Why do you always have to be so well behaved, so fair? Why don't you say, 'I loathe Vera with her damn high cheekbones and her long legs and her ponytail! I hate her acerbic wit! Let her wither, let her rot, I will come to you and freeze her out, I will take you from Vera forever, because I can, because I want to, because the idea of her repels me!'?

You would not say these things, and rarely allow yourself to feel these emotions. And I must remember that it is your private code of honour that I love about you. Doubtless your parents inculcated a sense of right in you, but it was the housemother at boarding school who taught you the dictum by which you live. 'Life is hell and there is no explanation for it,' she said, comforting you on your first sorrowful night away from home. 'That's why we must be kind to one another.'

I imagine how you fought with yourself to come to this compromise, this New Year's gift of a weekend for John. You read my mail and then went out quickly, driving to the burnt-out wind-break of the new workers' orchard. You stood there with replanting on your mind: Dutch alder or beefwood or Chilean poplar? But I kept coming through, blending with the smell of blackened wood all around: my letter, its tone of despair. Though you hardly know how to scheme and connive, it struck you that Theo's complaint about tatty curtains could be used to our advantage.

224

'What you need to do,' I imagine he said, 'is spend some money redecorating this place, instead of always running after your charity cases and mendicants.'

So you have lied to him, and I will join you there. Let us spend our days in the nature reserve, in the kloof where water drips over the rare disas, and only return to your house at night, like the thieves and vagabonds that we are.

I have twisted your righteousness. But, Theresa, I will make it all right again. I will never leave you, or switch off this light.

Yes, I've looked at those lines again. They could make a poem, you're right. I'll bring it when I come.

John Stuart Carson (1965-)
Should Old Acquaintance be Forgot?
Standing on some elegant balcony at sunset,
wearing a pretty dress and sparkling sandals,
you will raise your glass to his, and later,
when the New Year is counted in,
you and your friends will kiss each other
or shake hands.

Someone will take a photograph of you all,
with your prosperously raised glasses,
grouped around a table with a large platter
of fresh oysters as its centrepiece.

It is nothing,
or only a little thing,
or shall I say:
just one more link
in the chainsaw that keeps us apart.

Acknowledgements

The author and publisher gratefully acknowledge the following persons and instances for permission to quote copyright material:

'Child Burial' by Paula Meehan from *The Man Who Was Marked By Winter* (1991), by kind permission of the author; The Gallery Press, Loughcrew, Oldcastle, County Meath, Ireland and Wake Forest University Press, North Carolina. Mongane Wally Serote for permission to quote the first line of 'A Poem on Black and White', first published in *Tsetlo*. The quotation on page 202 reprinted with permission of Scribner, an imprint of Simon & Schuster Adult Publishing Group from *Cry, The Beloved Country* by Alan Paton. Copyright © 1948 by Alan Paton; copyright renewed © 1976 by Alan Paton. Charles Wright, excerpt from 'Reunion' in Country Music: Selected Early Poems; 2nd Ed. © 1991 by Charles Wright and reprinted by permission of Wesleyan University Press.

Every effort has been made to trace copyright holders or their assigns. The author and publisher apologise for any inadvertent infringement of copyright and, if this is drawn to their attention, will be pleased to make the necessary correction in any subsequent edition.